MY BOYFRIEND'S WIFE

Praise for Joy Argento

Exes and O's

"I really appreciated the new take on a burned lover in Ali. Instead of pushing love away forever, she decides to actively seek out what has gone wrong in order to do better in her future. I also enjoyed how the story focuses on what a healthy relationship should be and how to get to that. It was refreshing…If you're in the mood for a gentle second-chance romance that has just enough angst, great character development, and will have you dying for a donut, run for this book!"—*Lesbian Review*

Before Now

"*Before Now* by Joy Argento is a mixture of modern day romance and historical fiction…There was some welcome humour and a bit of angst. An interesting story well told." —*Kitty Kat's Book Review Blog*

Emily's Art and Soul

"…the leads are well rounded and credible. As a 'friends to lovers' romance the author skillfully transforms their budding friendship to an increasing intimacy. Mindy, Emily's Down syndrome sister, is a great secondary character, very realistic in her traits and interactions with other people. Her fresh outlook on life and her 'best friend' declarations help to keep the upbeat tone."—*LezReviewBooks*

"This was such a sweet book. Great story that would be perfect as a holiday read. The plot was fun and the pace really good. The protagonists were enjoyable and Emily's character was well fleshed out…This is the first book I've read by Joy Argento and it won't be the last. I'm looking forward to what comes next."—*Rainbow Literary Society*

By the Author

Emily's Art and Soul

Carrie and Hope

Before Now

No Regrets

Exes and O's

Missed Conception

Gin and Bear It

I do, I don't

Letters from Sarah

My Boyfriend's Wife

Visit us at www.boldstrokesbooks.com

MY BOYFRIEND'S WIFE

by

Joy Argento

2025

MY BOYFRIEND'S WIFE

ISBN 13: 978-1-63679-866-0

This Trade Paperback Original Is Published By
Bold Strokes Books, Inc.
P.O. Box 249
Valley Falls, NY 12185

First Edition: September 2025

Credits
Editor: Cindy Cresap
Production Design: Stacia Seaman
Cover Design by Tammy Seidick

For my readers. I love you all!

Chapter One

W hat the hell?" Megan mumbled as the ringing phone on her nightstand startled her out of a deep sleep. She turned over, tangling herself in the bed sheet, causing her frustration level to rise even higher. Dozer, her cat, jumped off the bed.

She didn't recognize the number on the caller ID. Her first impulse was to hit the end button, but she changed her mind when she realized it was a local area code. What if it was some kind of emergency involving her sister or dad? What else would it be at three thirty in the morning? Panic rose up her chest.

"Hello?" she said. She cleared her throat to try to dislodge some of the sleep her voice still held.

"You're a threat to my marriage," a female said.

Huh? What? Confusion added to the list of emotions Megan had experienced in the last two minutes. "Who is this?"

"You know damn well who this is." The caller's anger was evident even through the phone and Megan's groggy brain.

"Um, actually I don't."

"You've been screwing my husband for God knows how long."

Husband? Megan wasn't involved with anyone's husband. "I think you have the wrong number."

"Megan, right? You know Michael Foreman? Right again?"

"Actually, I don't." Mike Murry, her boyfriend, had left her bed two hours ago. His scent still lingered on her sheets. She had no idea who Michael Foreman was. But wait. This woman knew her name.

How—what—who? This wasn't making any sense. "How do you know my name and how did you get my number?"

"I got it off Michael's phone. He got home an hour and a half ago and I know he was with you. Don't try to deny it."

Megan sat up, roughly pulling the tangled sheet from her legs. "Wait. What? You said Michael Foreman?"

"I did," she said. "You heard me." Her voice broke, and Megan suspected she was close to crying.

"I don't know any Michael Foreman, but my boyfriend's name is Mike. Mike Murry."

"Oh my God."

"What? What's going on here?" Whatever it was, it was obviously very emotional to this woman.

"Murry is my maiden name."

"Um, I don't understand."

"Did your boyfriend tell you he's married?"

Married? Mike was married? Were they even talking about the same guy? "He's not married. I mean, no, he didn't say he was married. I'm confused here. Why don't you tell me what's going on."

It took all of three minutes for this woman to convince Megan that her boyfriend, Mike, was indeed her husband. That fucking, lying, cheating bastard.

"I didn't know he was married or anything about you," Megan explained. "I would never do that to another woman." More emotions coursed through her. Anger at Mike mixed with sympathy for his wife. "What's your name?" Megan asked.

She hesitated. "Tara." Her voice had softened considerably. She sounded defeated.

"Tara," Megan repeated. "Obviously Mike and I are over. Just so you know, we were only together for a couple of months." That sounded lame even to Megan's ears. She knew it only being a short amount of time wasn't going to ease Tara's pain. "What are you going to do?" Megan wasn't sure why she cared. Maybe it was the heartbreak in Tara's voice. Megan remembered how hurt she'd been after she found out her last girlfriend had cheated on her. That was almost five years ago, and it still stung. Yes, she was furious at Mike, but her feelings for him hadn't developed much past *the liking him* stage. Her concern now was for his wife, who he had obviously hurt badly. It didn't make much sense, but she didn't question it.

"I don't know. I don't think you're the first. I'm sure you're not. He's been disappearing and coming home late claiming he was at work for a couple of years now."

"I'm so sorry." Megan wasn't sure what else to say.

"You had no idea he was married?" Tara sniffed loudly, and Megan was sure she was crying. "Please tell me the truth."

Megan searched her mind. Did she have any clue? She needed to be as honest with herself as much as she felt the need to be honest with Tara.

No wedding ring or tan line on his ring finger. Never hesitated to stay late but never slept over, and Megan had never asked him to. Nothing that she could think of led her to think he was married. "No," she answered after running the last two months with him through her mind. "I had no idea."

There was silence on the other end of the phone for what seemed like an eternity. Megan pulled the phone from her ear to see if they were still connected.

"I've come right out and asked him if he was cheating on me," Tara finally said. "He denied it. I knew it was true in my heart. Now I know for sure."

"I'm sorry," Megan repeated.

"Okay. Um…well. Okay. Yeah. I'll let you go. Thanks for the information. Please don't tell Michael that we talked. I don't want him to know that I know—yet."

"Sure," Megan said, just as her phone beeped, indicating that Tara had already hung up.

"Well, that sucks," Megan said out loud to no one. She glanced around her room, not that she could see much in the dark. There wasn't anything in her apartment that belonged to Mike. They weren't at the place in their relationship where they were leaving stuff at each other's place. Not that Megan had ever been to his house. Now she knew why. She'd questioned him about it, of course. His explanation that he lived with his ailing mother—his very religious ailing mother—hadn't sat quite right with her, but she wasn't invested enough in the relationship to push it.

No, she wasn't that attached to him, and she hadn't asked herself why. Until now. Looking back, she realized that he hadn't been very invested either. He always seemed to have one foot out the door. She thought it was because he was an airline pilot and always on the go. He wasn't invested because he had already invested in someone else—Tara.

She didn't realize she was shaking until she put her head on her pillow. She closed her eyes, but sleep wasn't her friend. Turned out Mike wasn't her friend either.

Chapter Two

So, what are you going to do?" Cori asked. It had been her idea for them to meet for lunch at the Silver Spoon Café. She seemed to always know when Tara needed a friend. They preferred the outside seating in the summer, but that was never an option in October. It was far too cold for that with the weather in western New York.

Tara watched Cori sip her tea. She set the cup down and focused her eyes intently, waiting for a reply. They'd been best friends since first grade. That was unusual in this time when so many friendships seemed disposable. Cori was her maid of honor when she married Michael almost fourteen years ago. What a mistake that had been. She liked Michael, but she wasn't madly in love with him. At the age of twenty-two, she was still single and living at home with her parents. *They* were madly in love with him. No. That wasn't exactly right. They were madly in love with his money—the money he'd inherited from his parents. Tara looked at it more like an opportunity to get out of their house—away from the emotional abuse. If she had been wiser back then, she would have saved the money she made working at the donut shop during college and moved to her own place instead of getting married.

Cori cleared her throat. Loudly. "Um?"

Tara pushed her thoughts and regrets aside and concentrated on the question. "I don't know." She shook her head. "You know I have a prenup that says I get a good chunk of money if we get divorced because he cheats. My parents insisted on that. It's the one good thing they did."

Cori nodded. Tara had shared a lot of the emotional abuse she'd suffered at their hands. "And if you cheat, you get nothing," Cori added.

"I'm not the one cheating," she said a little too loudly. Two elderly women at the next table turned and looked at her before turning their attention back to their own conversation.

"Sorry. I know that. I wasn't implying that you are. Okay. So. Prenup. You have to prove he was cheating, right?"

"I'm not sure how to go about doing that. It's not like I have pictures of him and what's her name—Megan—together."

"This Megan woman admitted to sleeping with him, right?"

"More or less."

"Do you think she would be willing to testify in court?"

Tara let out a breath that came out in a huff. "There is no way I'm asking her to do that. I don't want anything to do with her." She pushed the plate with the apple pie she'd ordered away from her. Her appetite was gone. Not that she'd had much of one the last few months.

"What are your alternatives? If you don't get the money from the prenup, then what?"

Tara shook her head. "I don't know. I mean, I'll continue working, but I don't make a ton of money as a preschool teacher. I would have enough to live on, but not enough to continue helping Anna pay for Brandon's care. There is no way I can help her without that money." Things had been so hard for her younger—and only— sister, Anna, since losing her husband three years ago.

"How is Brandon doing, by the way?"

Tara was grateful for the change in subject, although she knew it would be brief. "He's about the same as the last time you saw him. He seems to enjoy being around other kids. But it's hard to tell with him sometimes. I swear his autism got worse when his dad died."

"I agree," Cori said. "How old is he now?"

"Thirteen. Hard to believe. Seems like he was a baby only yesterday."

"Have you thought about hiring a PI?"

And there they were. Back to the topic at hand. "I don't have enough money for a private investigator. And I can't use the money in our joint account without Michael knowing. He's been very careful with the money and watching what I spend it on. Of course, I had no idea he was spending it on mistresses."

"I hate how controlling he is over you."

Tara sighed. She'd gone from controlling parents to a controlling marriage. At least Michael wasn't abusive—unless you counted neglect as abuse. She knew Cori counted it.

"That brings us back to the woman he was sleeping with. You need her to testify."

"Even if I asked her to help me, why would she?"

"Why wouldn't she? She was also betrayed by Michael. She must be pretty pissed off too."

Tara tossed the idea around in her mind. Would she be willing to help Megan out if their roles were reversed? She wasn't sure. And she had no idea how to go about asking Megan—that was, if she decided to ask her at all. No. She couldn't do that.

"So…"

"I don't think I can ask her to help me. I need to figure out another way to prove Michael cheated."

"I don't think there is another way. I can call her if you want."

Tara tilted her head and squinted her eyes until Cori was nothing but a blur. She needed to block everything out except the question. Should she ask Megan for help? She let the question bounce around in her mind.

"I can see the wheels turning and there's that burnt rubber smell coming from your ears. How's it going in there?" Cori pointed to Tara's head.

Tara had no idea how much time had passed when Cori brought her out of her thoughts. She shook her head.

"Maybe the thing to do is talk to your lawyer about it."

Tara let out a sarcastic laugh. "My lawyer? My lawyer is Michael's lawyer. I don't have my own and I'm sure as hell not going to tip my hand to his."

"Maybe the thing to do is *find* a lawyer."

Tara smiled. "That's why I keep you around. You always have the best advice. I adore you."

"I know. Everybody should."

"You mean they don't?"

"Not everyone. Yet. But I'm working on it."

Tara jumped at the sound of the waiter's voice beside her. She'd been so focused on Cori that she hadn't noticed him approaching. "Anything wrong with the pie?" he asked, pointing to Tara's untouched plate.

"Hard to tell," Cori volunteered. "She hasn't eaten a single bite." She raised her eyebrows while staring directly into Tara's eyes.

Tara didn't appreciate the remark and tried to convey the feeling with her expression. She wasn't sure if it landed, because Cori continued. "No, it's fine. I'll do my best to get her to eat it. And if she doesn't, I promise, I will."

"Is there anything else I can get for you?" the waiter asked, directing the question to Cori.

"No, but we appreciate you asking." She gave him a flirty smile.

Tara didn't bother looking at him to see if he smiled back. She knew he did. They all did. Cori could have her choice of men. They all chased her. She'd let Marcus catch her. They'd been married for three glorious years—her words. That didn't stop her from flirting. Marcus didn't seem to mind. He knew she'd never cheat. And he was right.

That brought Tara's thoughts back to *her* cheating husband—and whether asking Megan for help was a good idea.

"Maybe it is," she said.

"Excuse me?" the waiter asked her.

She hadn't realized he was still there.

"Nothing," she responded. "I'm just thinking out loud."

"A good idea to ask Megan?" Cori asked.

"Who's Megan?" Why was the waiter still standing there asking questions that were none of his business?

"You should do it," Cori said, ignoring him.

Tara looked up at him. "We're all set," she said, hoping he would leave. What the hell was wrong with men? She knew that wasn't a fair question. At the moment, she didn't care. Michael had betrayed her and their marriage vows. Her father had been less than nurturing while she was growing up and not very supportive of her now. He seemed to like Michael more than he liked her. *Well, he can have him. I hope they're very happy together.* The ridiculous thought made her smile. It felt strange. She couldn't remember the last time she smiled. Not a real smile anyway.

She knew you couldn't rely on another person to make you happy, but she was learning that another person sure could make you miserable.

"Um." Oh my God, the waiter still hadn't left.

"We are all set," Cori repeated, without looking at him. She seemed to have all her attention focused on Tara. He turned and silently skulked away. "I thought he'd never leave. Now tell me what you were talking about."

"What?"

"You said 'maybe it is.' Or something like that."

Tara had to sort through the last round of thoughts to try to remember why'd she said that. "Oh yeah. I was thinking about what you said about Megan. Asking her, I mean."

"You should."

"You said that."

"And I was right. I usually am. And humble too."

"You are." She paused. "And I'm thinking it might be my only way to prove Michael cheated. I'm just not sure she would do it, though."

"There is only one way to find out. Ask her."

Tara rubbed the back of her neck. *Ask her.* That was easier said than done.

Chapter Three

"I don't understand," Michael said.

"It's just not working for me," Megan responded into the phone. There was no way she was going to break up with him in person. She'd done her best to avoid him altogether for the past several days. He'd called no less than seven times before she'd answered the phone with the words *it's over*.

"Why? I thought things were going well."

She was tempted to say because he was a lying, cheating fucker, but Tara had asked her not to tell him that she knew. Her mind scrambled for an answer. "I've met someone else." It wasn't a total lie. She'd met his wife over the phone. She put her feet up on the coffee table and leaned back against the couch.

There were several long moments of silence. Megan was about to hang up when Michael finally spoke.

"What?" He sounded pissed.

"It is what it is."

"I hate that phrase, and it isn't an answer. This is bullshit." Yep. He was pissed.

This was a side of Michael she hadn't seen before. And why would she have? Up until now he'd gotten what he wanted. He'd gotten her into bed. She wasn't sure how to respond. She knew he was a cheater. She didn't know if he could be violent. She didn't think so.

"I'm sorry," he said, when she didn't respond. His tone was much softer. "You just mean so much to me, baby. I don't want to lose you."

She recognized the manipulation tactic. She'd heard it over and over again from Aliza after she'd caught her cheating. *But, baby, I love you. But, baby, I'll never do it again. But, baby...* She wasn't falling for that. Ever. Again.

"I'm sorry," she mumbled. "I've got to go."

"Hey—" Michael started as she hung up the phone, got up, and threw it on the couch that she'd just vacated.

She wasn't surprised when he called her back immediately. She blocked his number after the fifth time. He was nothing if not persistent. Actually, he was less than nothing.

As a stress eater she'd stocked her apartment with comfort food a couple of days before. She moved the container of milk out of her way to reach the peanut butter pie in the back of her fridge. She cut a large slice, plated it up, grabbed a fork, and headed back to the living room.

"What the hell?" she said, when her phone rang for a sixth time. She was relieved to see that it was her sister. "Hey, Jilly." She sat on the couch and put the plate on the coffee table in front of her. Dozer jumped up on her lap and she mindlessly stroked his silky black fur. He purred his appreciation.

"You know I hate it when you call me that," Jill said.

"That's why I do it."

"Butthead. Whatcha up to today?"

"Well, let's see. I just broke up with Michael, so, um…I'm totally free."

"What? Why? I never even had a chance to meet him."

"And you probably never would have. Turns out he has a wife."

"Oh shit. How did you find out?" Jill asked.

"She called me."

"No way."

"Way." Megan told her about the late-night call from Tara.

"I repeat—oh shit."

"Yep. Did you want to do something today? Is that why you called?" She used her finger to swipe at the whipped cream on the pie and put it in her mouth, avoiding Dozer's attempts at licking it.

Oh yeah. That hit the spot. She was already starting to feel better. It probably wasn't a good thing to like comfort food so much. *Okay, okay. Junk food. Call it what it is.* It didn't matter. If it helped relax her, she didn't want to think about that.

"This is the last farmers market on Long Pond Road for the season. Wanna go? Harper said she would love to see you."

"Harper, huh? When did she start talking?"

"A year ago."

Megan laughed. "She's only eleven months old. She started talking a month before she was born?"

"She's very advanced."

"She must take after me, then." Another swipe of the whipped cream made it into her mouth.

"Okay. We can go with that theory if you agree to go with us. It's just so much easier with two people."

"In other words, your husband didn't want to go with you, so you thought you would hit me up."

"How dare you. I called you because you're my sister and I love you very much. I just wanted the pleasure of your company." She paused. "That and my husband is going bowling, and if you come with us you can help with Harper."

"Well, how can I say no to that?"

"You can't. I'll pick you up in thirty minutes. Be ready."

"Okay," Megan whined. "If I must."

"You must. See you soon."

Megan hit the end button on her phone. She reconsidered eating the peanut butter pie, knowing it might not sit well in her stomach if she was walking around, possibly carrying her niece. Jill always brought a stroller, but sometimes Harper just plain objected to being in it and Megan often ended up carrying her.

One more swipe of the whipped cream with her finger. She ate half of it and let Dozer lick the rest before she put the pie back in the refrigerator. Spending time with her sister and niece would be just as good as comfort food to cheer her up.

Just as she said, Jill arrived exactly thirty minutes later. Megan grabbed a light jacket, told Dozer she'd see him later, locked her apartment door behind her, and headed down the flight of stairs that led to the outside door.

"Shh." Jill put her finger to her lips as Megan slipped into the passenger seat. "Harper fell asleep five seconds after I put her in the car." She pointed to the car seat in the back as if Megan wouldn't know where Harper was.

"That kid could sleep through a bomb blast," Megan whispered.

Jill pushed a chunk of hair away from her face. It looked a couple shades lighter than it was the last time Megan had seen her. Her natural dark brown hair used to be the same color as Megan's. She started coloring it as soon as she spotted a couple of gray hairs creeping in a few years ago. She wasn't happy about the fact that Megan, who was three years older than her, didn't have a gray hair on her head. "Not lately," Jill whispered back. "She wakes up at the slightest sound." Almost as if on cue, Harper started crying.

Megan put up her hands. "I didn't do it."

"She might go back to sleep again once we are driving," Jill said.

She didn't. She did, however, calm down a few minutes later. Jill pulled into an empty parking space—apparently the last one available—and Megan got Harper out of her car seat.

"Well, hello there, little lady. How's my favorite niece?"

"She's your only niece." Jill opened the hatchback and lugged out a stroller. She had it unfolded and set up in less than a minute. The few times Megan had tried to do that she'd given up. Baby things were so complicated these days. She could understand having a canopy to keep the sun off the kid, but why did a baby need cup holders and a million compartments to hold thing?. She watched with fascination as Jill put several diapers, baby wipes, teething toys, and pacifiers into the compartments. She put a plastic cup into the cup holder and filled it with Cheerios from a large ziplock bag. Maybe there was a reason for all those things.

"All set," Jill said. She reached out for Harper and strapped her in.

"You're so good at that," Megan said. She tied her jacket around her waist. The sun was warming up the day more than she thought it would.

"Did you just pay me a compliment?" Jill started walking toward the vendor area.

"It was an accident," Megan responded with a smile.

By the time they made their way back to the car, Megan was glad the stroller had so many compartments. It saved her from carrying all the goodies she'd bought. While Jill's purchases included mostly fresh fruit and vegetables, Megan's consisted of a huge bag of kettle corn, a box of pastries, and several kinds of homemade fudge. Okay, okay, she did break down and buy a pint of fresh figs. But figs tasted like candy, so they were still comfort food.

"Want to come in?" Megan asked as Jill pulled into the parking lot of her apartment building.

"No. I appreciate the offer, but I want to get home and get Harper settled. Her ten-minute nap on the way here wasn't long enough. She's going to get really cranky if she doesn't get a good nap in."

"Understood. Thanks for including me in your day." She opened the car door.

"How are you, really? I mean since the breakup with Michael?"

Megan closed the door and turned to face her sister. "Technically I only broke up with him today. I've known that he was married for a few days. It was a shock for sure. I had no clue. I'm not sure I've totally dealt with it yet in my head." She stopped and thought about it for a moment. "I think my heart's fine. I wasn't in love with him or anything. I did have hopes that my feelings were going to head in that direction, but they hadn't. He treated me good. But I guess the mistress always gets treated good."

"Mistress," Jill repeated. "I hadn't thought of that. But I guess if he's married, that fits."

"Yep. I have to say I feel worse for his wife than I do for me. I mean, I know what it feels like to be cheated on. It sucks. And from what she said, I'm not the first. Which makes him a total scumbag. So, to answer your question, I guess I'm doing okay."

Jill leaned in and gave her a tight squeeze. "I'm here if you need me." She pulled back. "Now get out of my car so I can get my kid home." She winked. "Love ya, sis."

"Love you too." Megan retrieved her purchases from the back of the car. Harper smiled at her from her car seat. "Love you too, kiddo." She shut the hatchback, maneuvering her bags from one hand to the other so she didn't drop anything.

She turned as she approached the apartment building door and tipped up her chin at her sister. She had been glad for the company and the distraction—and now she had plenty of goodies to help further distract her.

She fumbled with her keys at her apartment door, determined not to drop anything, when her phone vibrated in her back pocket. It stopped by the time she got the door unlocked and her packages on the kitchen table. It pinged, notifying her that there was a voice mail.

She put it on speaker and hit the button. "Um…Um…Yeah. This is Tara. Um Tara Foreman. Michael's wife. Can you give me a call back? Please. I would really appreciate it."

Dozer jumped up on the table, a move that often got him in trouble. But Megan was too distracted to bother reprimanding him. "Huh. That's weird. I wonder if she wants to know if I'm still seeing him," she said, more to herself than Dozer. "I'm not, in case you're wondering." This time she did address the cat. "I guess I should call her back and reassure her that he's all hers—until he finds his next victim. Guys like that never change. He should be neutered."

Dozer let out a loud meow. "Oh, sorry. I know. Sore subject for you." He jumped off the table when Megan poured fresh cat food into his dish. She plopped down on the couch in the living room and called Tara back.

"Hello," Tara answered on the first ring.

"Hi. It's Megan. You called? I want to reassure you—"

"I have a huge favor to ask you," Tara interrupted. "Could you—I mean would you consider helping me?" She paused.

"Okay. With what?" Megan asked when Tara didn't continue.

"Would you consider testifying in court that you were involved with Michael?"

"Why? Don't we live in a no-fault divorce state? You don't have to prove infidelity to divorce him."

"It's a little more complicated than that. If I may explain." She sounded nervous and tearful.

"Of course. Go on."

"Megan, I think you are the latest in a long string of affairs. I'm done putting up with it. We have a prenup, and adultery means I get a large settlement. I can take him to the cleaners for what he's done to me." She hesitated. "I shouldn't have said it that way. I need the money because I help my sister pay for her son's private school. He has autism, and the public school just wasn't cutting it for him."

"Um," Megan said. "What can I do to help?" She had no idea why she was even asking, but something in Tara's voice made her want to ease her pain. "I mean, we can confront him together. That way he can't deny it if we are both standing in front of him."

Silence.

"Tara?"

"I don't know. I…" She let the words drift off.

"No. It was a dumb idea. I'm sorry."

"I don't want him to know anything yet. It might be better to bring all this up when I divorce him. I need to think about this."

"Are you sure that's something you want to do? Divorce is so—I don't know—final."

"I'm sure. I'm done with him. I never should have married him. Long story, but it was the biggest mistake of my life."

"Then how should we do this?" Megan asked.

"I have no idea. I don't even have a lawyer yet. Do you have any suggestions?"

Megan couldn't help but laugh. "Sorry, I know it's not funny. I don't mean to make light of this. It's just that this is my first time helping my boyfriend's wife divorce him. Ex-boyfriend. I want you to know that I told him it's over."

"You didn't tell him we talked, did you?" Tara asked.

"No. You asked me not to and I didn't. He didn't take it too well."

"That would explain his crappy mood this afternoon."

"I'm sorry if I made things harder for you," Megan said. She wasn't sure why she felt the need to apologize. She wanted to ease Tara's pain. She knew what it was like to be cheated on and have your heart ripped out by a partner.

"None of this is your fault. You didn't know he was married. This is all on him. Would you be willing to meet me so we can brainstorm some ideas? I mean, I know this is a crazy thing to ask. I wouldn't blame you if you told me to go to hell."

Megan's heart opened a little more toward Tara. No woman

should have to go through this. "I would never tell you that. I'm more than willing to help. Just tell me when and where." She didn't know if she was looking forward to actually meeting Tara or terrified at the prospect.

Chapter Four

Megan searched the coffee shop for someone fitting the description Tara had given her. When she didn't see her, she approached the counter and ordered a bottle of water. Coffee would just add to the nerves that were already coursing through her like a runaway train.

"Megan?"

She jumped at the sound of her name spoken so close behind her. She whipped around, almost dropping the five-dollar bill she was about to hand the guy behind the counter.

"I'm so sorry," the woman said. "I didn't mean to startle you."

Tara had described herself as five foot four, having light brown hair, and wearing a light blue shirt. She had failed to mention the auburn hue in her full wavy hair, her deep blue eyes, full lips, and beautiful face—edging toward gorgeous. Megan felt less-than in her presence. How could anyone in their right mind cheat on her? Mike was such an ass.

"Megan?" Tara repeated. She hesitated. "Or not?" She looked around.

Megan realized she hadn't responded and probably had her mouth hanging open. "Yeah. Yes. Um. I mean yes, I'm Megan. Sorry." How many more times could she say that word?

An unexpected smile spread across Tara's face, revealing a set of perfect teeth. Something pinged at Megan's heart—or was it her libido? What the hell? This was Michael's wife. Lying. Cheating. Shithead. Michael.

"What can I get for you?" Megan said to cover how flustered she felt. "Coffee? Latte? A brownie?"

"A brownie," Tara responded. "If you'll share it with me. And a cappuccino. But this is my treat. It's the least I could do seeing as you're willing to help me. At least I hope you're still willing to."

Megan nodded, then shook her head. "You don't have to do that. Pay for it, I mean." She needed to get her head back on her shoulders. She wasn't sure she was making sense.

"Anything else?" the young guy behind the counter asked. He moved the bottle of water he had set on the counter closer to Megan.

She turned her attention back to him. "Yes—" she started.

"Medium vanilla cappuccino, the biggest brownie you have, and whatever else this lovely lady would like," Tara interrupted.

"Just the water," Megan mumbled.

Tara seemed like she was about to object, and Megan assumed she was going to tell her to get more than just water, but she stopped and handed her credit card to the kid.

They retrieved their orders and Megan followed Tara to a small table in the corner. Several long moments passed before either of them spoke.

"Have some brownie," Tara said as she pushed the plate closer to Megan. She placed one of the two forks she had on the edge of the plate.

Megan couldn't help but laugh. This whole thing seemed ludicrous. The wife of her boyfriend—former boyfriend—had just offered her a brownie. And the brownie did look delish.

Tara took her own fork, cut off a piece of brownie, and put it in her mouth. Megan avoided watching the whole endeavor and looked directly into Tara's eyes instead. That turned out to be even more dangerous. She felt herself get lost in them and blinked against the feelings it invoked in her. What the actual hell?

"Do you think we should confront Michael now, or wait until I take him to court?" Tara asked.

"Huh?"

Tara repeated the question.

"What do you think?" Megan asked. "I mean, I've never been in this situation before." She paused. "Actually, I've been where you are. Not married. But my ex-girlfriend cheated on me. And I know how much it hurts." She waited for Tara to respond to the word *girlfriend*. She didn't.

"I'm so sorry," Tara said, and Megan could tell she meant it.

"Me too. About Michael. I never would have—if—if—I'd have known—"

"I know. I don't think you'd be sitting here with me otherwise."

Megan nodded. "So, what should we do?"

"Maybe go to his work and confront him in front of his coworkers. Have witnesses," Tara said.

"At the airport?"

"Airport?"

Megan shook her head. "He told me he's a pilot. That was a lie, wasn't it?" She didn't wait for a response. "The perfect excuse to be gone for days at a time, huh?"

"I'm not surprised. He seems to be a professional liar. He works in an office downtown."

"I wonder what else he told me that wasn't true." She shook her head. "I would be willing to bet that none of it was." She cleared her throat. "Does he have a sick mother he helps take care of when he's in town?" She paused. "Wait. He's not a pilot, so he doesn't leave town on a regular basis."

"No. He doesn't. Both his parents died a long time ago."

Megan's stomach did a flip. Shit. How did she fall for all his lies? It made her question her ability to judge people—their character. Mike had presented himself as an upstanding, caring, generous gentleman. And she fell for it.

"Stop," Tara said, interrupting her thoughts.

Megan was confused. "What?"

"Stop thinking this is somehow your fault for believing him."

"How did you do that? Can you read minds?" Megan laughed.

"Yes. It's my superpower. One of many." She took another bite of the brownie and sipped her cappuccino. "Apparently, my superpowers failed when it came to Michael. Although I've suspected his infidelity for a while now. I just didn't have proof."

Megan put her elbow on the table and her chin on her hand. "Can you fly?"

"What?"

"Your superpowers. You can read minds. Can you fly? If I could have any superpower, it would be the ability to fly."

"No. Most of my superpowers are secret. I don't usually tell people that I can read minds. It freaks them out. You just happened to figure it out."

Megan smiled. She wasn't sure what to expect when she agreed to meet with Tara, but this conversation sure wasn't it.

"You haven't touched your half of this brownie," Tara said. She took another sip of her cappuccino. "If I were to read your mind again, I would say that it's because of nerves. I have a feeling you like sweets."

Megan knew she had a few extra pounds on her. Normally, she didn't care, and didn't care about other people's opinions of her. But for some reason, she didn't want Tara to think less of her. "Are you referring to my weight?" she said, trying to make light of it.

"Oh my God, no. I was just joking around. There's nothing wrong with your weight. I'm so sorry if you thought that's what I meant."

That eased Megan's mind. "You're right. I am nervous. Well, I was. Not so much now. And I do like sweets. Your superpower is still working."

"Good to know. Now what I don't know is how to proceed with this divorce stuff."

"Did you find a lawyer yet?" Megan eyed the brownie and the walnuts sprinkled on top. It did look good, and her anxiety had settled down. She took a bite and let the chocolate coat her tongue. It tasted as good as it looked.

"No. Not yet. I wanted to talk to you first. Kind of see where this is going. I guess to see if you're on my side." Was that a blush creeping up Tara's neck? Megan was pretty sure it was.

"I am. I'll do whatever you want me to do." Tara's blush deepened, confusing Megan.

Tara cleared her throat. "I appreciate that. You don't always get what you want. But you always get what you need."

"What?"

Tara shook her head. "Nothing. My best friend always says that. I don't know why I just said it." She'd spent most of her life not getting what she wanted. Had she gotten what she needed? She'd needed to get out of her parents' house, and Michael was what she needed to do that. She needed to help her sister, and again, Michael was what she needed. Did she still need him? She needed some of his money to continue helping her sister and to get her own life back on track.

"I have a great story about getting what you need," Megan said, interrupting her thoughts.

Tara brought her eyes up to Megan's. She saw nothing but kindness there. She was appalled to find her own eyes tearing up. She hadn't experienced a whole lot of kindness in her life, especially from a total stranger—a stranger that by all accounts should have been her enemy, not acting like a friend. She blinked several times to try to keep the tears from cascading down her cheeks. If Megan noticed, she didn't say anything.

"Do you remember when we had that major snowstorm a few years ago?" She didn't wait for a response. "We had over three feet of snow dropped on us overnight. I had spent the night at my girlfriend's house, and we both needed to get to work." She paused.

Tara wondered if Megan was waiting for a response. About the snowstorm? About the fact that she'd had a girlfriend? Tara didn't know, so she just nodded.

"There was no way we were going to be able to get someone to plow us out, so we decided the only thing to do was shovel the massive amount of snow blocking us in. But—" Megan smiled as if the memory made her happy.

Tara couldn't help but smile in return. "Sounds like quite the task."

"It was, but to make things even worse, we couldn't find the snow shovels. Turned out that her nephews had used them to shovel off the pond behind her house the day before so they could ice skate. The only thing we could find was a small garden shovel. Anyway, we set to work, figuring it would take us hours. The town had plowed the road, but there was almost no traffic. A single truck drove by and something flew out of the bed of it. Obviously, the driver had no idea he'd lost something because he never slowed down or came back for it."

"What was it?" Tara's curiosity was piqued. She wasn't sure if it was the story itself, or the way Megan was telling it. She was animated. Smiling.

"A snow shovel."

"No way," Tara said.

"Way." Megan paused. "The lesson here is that the Universe doesn't always give you what you want, but it always gives you what you need. And let me tell you—we needed a snow shovel. I mean, a snowblower would have been better. But that shovel was mighty appreciated."

Tara couldn't help but laugh. She also couldn't help but like Megan. "Wow. That's a true story?"

Megan held up her hand, letting her fingers separate between her middle and ring fingers. "Scout's honor."

Tara laughed. "I believe that is the Vulcan salute for live long and prosper. I take it you were never a Boy Scout?"

"Never. Not a Girl Scout either. More into 4-H and raising chickens. We didn't have a hand signal or even a secret handshake."

"You raised chickens?" Tara asked. "Did you live on a farm?"

"Chicken," Megan corrected her. "No farm. Just a single chicken. Jennifer."

Tara wasn't so sure about this story, although she had no reason to doubt Megan. She seemed to be truthful and trustworthy—so far. "You had a chicken, and you named her Jennifer?"

"What else would you name a chicken? She looked like Jennifer Aniston. Well, she had Jennifer Aniston's hairstyle, anyway."

Tara laughed. "Now I know you're lying." She took a sip of her cappuccino, finishing it.

Megan shook her head. "I'm not. Wait…" She pulled her phone from her back pocket and tapped on it several times. She turned the phone toward Tara. "See?"

Tara looked at the photo of a chicken that Megan had obviously pulled up on Google. It did look like it had hair. Tara wasn't sure it looked like Jennifer Aniston. "Polish non-bearded, white-crested cuckoo cockerel. I don't know. Looks more like Richard Simmons to me."

Megan scoffed. "Who ever heard of a chicken named Richard? That's just crazy." She slipped the phone back into her pocket.

"No. You're right. Jennifer is a much better name." She wondered if she should bring the conversation back to the reason they were meeting—Michael and his lying, cheating ways. Somehow, she didn't want to. She was actually enjoying their banter. It was so unexpected. "Whatever happened to her?"

"We ate her," Megan said, with a totally straight face, then burst out laughing.

"Did you just make that whole story up?" Her attempt to not laugh along didn't work, and her laugh came out more like a snort. She covered her mouth with her hand, embarrassed.

Megan didn't seem to notice. "Only the part about eating her. I really did have a pet chicken named Jennifer. My parents took her to live on a farm when she got older."

"A farm? Isn't that what parents tell kids when…" Tara hesitated. "You know. You know?"

"When the pet dies, you mean?"

Tara regretted saying anything. "Yeah. Sorry."

"Jennifer really did go live on a farm. We went to visit her a few times. She seemed happy."

"How can you tell if a chicken is happy?" Tara asked in earnest.

"By the big ol' smile on her little chicken face, of course."

Tara facepalmed. "Of course. How stupid of me." She couldn't believe what a nice—and unexpected—time she was having. "You know," she said, "I don't think we should confront Michael. Not yet anyway. I think we need the element of surprise. We don't want him to put his guard up and come up with excuses." She was almost sorry she'd changed the subject back to him, but at some point they needed to actually figure this out.

From the look that crossed Megan's face, she surmised that Megan was sorry for the change in direction too. Then as quickly as that look had appeared, it disappeared, and Megan's face softened. "I'm so sorry. Talking about chickens and such. Of course we need to get back to the subject at hand."

"No need to apologize. I have enjoyed our conversation. I just don't want to keep you from getting back to your life."

"You aren't keeping me away from anything. And to be totally honest with you, I've enjoyed talking to you too. I was really nervous about meeting you. I didn't know if you wanted to punch me in the face or something, and I wouldn't have blamed you if you did."

Tara smiled. "I'm pretty sure you could take me in a fight. I didn't want to risk it."

"I'm better at running than fighting. So you would have had to catch me first." She smiled back.

There was an awful lot of smiling going on, Tara realized. "I'm glad it didn't come to blows—or running. I try not to run unless I'm running from the police."

"Do you do that often?" Megan asked.

For some reason they continued to stray from the topic of Michael. Seemed like neither of them wanted to talk about him. "Only when I've stolen something. And no. I don't do that often. I'm kidding, of course." She paused. "I steal all the time." Another pause. "Kidding again. I don't steal at all." She hoped that Megan would find this funny. She wasn't sure why. Maybe because she liked seeing her smile.

Megan did more than smile. She laughed out loud. "That's good. Stealing is not a good habit to get into." She helped herself to another bite of brownie. "So, you were saying we shouldn't confront Michael. Go on."

Damn. She knew they needed to get back to that. Why didn't she want to? "Yeah. Let me talk to a lawyer first…as soon as I find one. Then we can figure out the best plan of attack."

"Sounds good to me. Just let me know when you know something." Another bite of brownie.

Tara was so grateful for Megan's willingness to help, and she actually looked forward to seeing her again. Who would have ever thought things would turn out that way?

❖

That went far better than I could have ever imagined, Tara thought as she slid into her car. Megan seemed willing—eager, in fact—to help her. When she'd made that late night phone call, it was with the intent to confront her and find out the truth. She had never expected to find an ally in Megan. *And* she had mentioned an ex-girlfriend. That was a surprise. Tara had to stop herself from admitting that she leaned that way as well. There was no sense outing herself now. She'd kept that secret to herself since seventh grade, when she realized she was head over heels for her best friend. She'd admitted it out loud only once in her life. Two years ago, Cori had listened quietly, asked a few questions, and given Tara a reassuring hug. They hadn't talked about it since. No, outing herself to a stranger now was not a good idea. She was glad she resisted the urge to blurt it out.

She smiled to herself. Michael was going to be in for a big surprise. She found that all she wanted at this point was to get what she felt she deserved. It wasn't a revenge thing. She was pissed, sure. But any love that she'd had for Michael—if she'd ever really loved him at all—was long gone. He'd chipped away at her heart until there was nothing left of it. At least nothing left for him.

She pulled into her driveway and was disappointed to see Michael's car. He wasn't usually home on a Sunday afternoon. Of course, Megan had broken up with him and he didn't have another girlfriend, as far as Tara knew. She also knew, without a doubt, that it wouldn't take him long to find a new one. She was still thinking about Megan as she went into the house. Yes, Tara was very grateful for Megan's help. She couldn't have picked a better person for her husband to cheat with. She laughed out loud at the thought.

"What's so funny?"

The sound of Michael's voice startled her. She hadn't noticed him sitting on the couch.

"Nothing," she said, turning around. She didn't want to be in the same space as him but didn't want to tip him off that anything was up. "Oh," she said. "You're home. I thought maybe you would be out with your…" She hesitated. "Buddies. Playing cards or something." She knew it sounded lame.

"I need to go to work at seven," he said. "Big meeting."

Bullshit, Tara thought. There weren't big meetings on a Sunday evening. Probably going to a bar to find his next conquest. She briefly considered following him but then thought better of it. She would have enough ammo with Megan's help. She didn't need to lower herself to his level. She thought back to her wedding day. The wedding her parents basically forced her into. Not basically. They bullied her into it.

Of course, they didn't know her predisposition for liking— loving—women. And there was no way Tara was ever going to tell them. The prospect of hell was a very real thing for them, and they'd pounded that into Tara's head since she was an infant. *If you don't eat all your dinner when there are starving children in this world, you will go straight to hell when you die. If you disobey us and go to that boy's party, you will go to hell. If you cut your hair short, people will think you're a lesbian. And lesbians go to hell.*

Well, she'd spent most of her life in hell. First with them and then with Michael. It hadn't started out bad. Not at all. Michael took her to expensive restaurants, on luxury cruises, to plays and movies. She enjoyed herself and she could tolerate the sex. It was pleasant enough. When he asked her to marry him, she'd turned him down at first. Her parents were furious at her. The verbal abuse escalated until she relented. At least it was a way to get away from them.

As the years went by, Michael became more and more distant. He spent more and more time away from the house—and away from her. She'd searched her mind to see if she'd done something wrong—treated him poorly or acted differently than she previously had. She concluded that she hadn't. She rarely refused him sex, made meals he liked, offered to accompany him to the college football games he was so fond of. She hadn't changed. He had. Or maybe he hadn't. Maybe he had been cheating on her from the start and she was just too stupid to see it. No. Not stupid. She could hear Cori's voice in her head, telling her to stop putting herself down. Too blinded by—not by love. Maybe by commitment. Even though her heart hadn't belonged to Michael, she had been determined to make this marriage work.

She'd ignored her feelings for women, locked them away in a box that she'd buried deep in her heart, where the rust and the moths couldn't get them. Sure, they popped up every now and then, when she saw a beautiful woman or watched a movie where women were lovers. Or in her dreams. Often in her dreams. She'd wake with a longing she couldn't satisfy. A fire she couldn't put out.

Michael didn't bother asking her where she'd been. She didn't expect him to. He didn't seem to have much interest in her these days. She'd heard or read somewhere that men that had affairs often treated their wives better out of a sense of guilt. That certainly wasn't the case with Michael. Maybe he didn't feel guilty about running around on her. Or maybe he just didn't care anymore. Either way, it didn't matter. They would be over soon, and she wouldn't have to think about it anymore.

She changed out of her nice clothes and into her jeans and a T-shirt. She hadn't wanted to look too casual when she met with Megan. Megan seemed nice enough. She sure was pretty. She could see why Michael took an interest in her. Her cute pixie-style dark hair framed her face perfectly, and her green eyes sparkled when she smiled, setting off a set of dimples that made you want to smile back. Tara had always been partial to dimples. Apparently, Michael was too. Funny, she thought, maybe we have the same taste in women. We should have been buddies, picking up women together, instead of a married couple.

She was surprised to find so much amusement in these troubling times. She found Megan amusing. That shocked her. She wasn't sure what to expect, but it certainly wasn't that.

Michael stuck his head in the bedroom door. "I'm heading out. I'm going to meet up with Tony for a drink before the meeting." As quickly as he appeared, he disappeared, and Tara heard him close the front door behind him.

She was glad to be alone. She looked around the bedroom, and a sadness overtook her. Yes, she would be rid of Michael, but she would also lose the home she'd come to love. It had been her safe haven after leaving her parents' house. She could fight for it in the divorce, of course. But she knew she wouldn't do that. This house was as much Michael's as it was hers—more so financially.

There were so many layers to ending a relationship. Tara knew she'd only scratched the surface of all the emotions that were ahead for her.

❖

Megan found herself excited—was that the right word?—at the prospect of helping Tara. Maybe it was excitement at the prospect of spending more time with Tara *while* helping her. What the hell was wrong with her? This woman was the wife of her former boyfriend. A married woman—currently at least. And obviously straight. Megan knew she shouldn't be attracted to her. But she couldn't help herself.

She found she was restless when she got home. A normal Sunday evening might include dinner—usually at her apartment—with Mike and then a little action in bed before he had to go home to his sick mother. His sick mother who had, according to Tara, died a long time ago.

It wasn't that she needed a partner, male or female, in her life. She'd spent plenty of time single between Cheating Aliza and dating Mike. Cheating Mike—Michael, as Tara had called him. She wasn't sure where the restlessness was coming from. This wasn't like her. Her mind kept returning to her conversation with Tara. She needed to stop this. It was ridiculous and she knew it.

Work. That's what she could do. She called Victoria, her business partner. They hosted a podcast together called *And Now This*, where they discussed mostly current events. It had gone from a local talk radio show to a national podcast with quite a few sponsors. They weren't rich—yet. But they earned enough to pay their bills and put food on the table.

"Hey," Victoria answered in her usual way.

"What are you doing? Want to go over some ideas for upcoming shows?"

"I was just about to feed Jeramy," Victoria said, referring to her four-year-old. "I can call you back when he's in bed if you want."

Megan knew that would be sometime after eight o'clock if he didn't give his mother a hard time—which he often did. "No. That's okay. I was just bored. I'll do some research online and we can just get together at the regular time on Monday."

"Are you sure?" Victoria asked.

"Yep. Go take care of your kid."

"Okay. See ya."

Megan grabbed her laptop from her desk in the spare bedroom

she used as an office and settled on the couch with it. Dozer jumped up and plopped himself on top of the computer before she had a chance to open it. "Hey," she said. "It's really hard to work with you in my way."

He looked up at her and rolled onto his back, content to stay there. She scratched his belly and he purred his appreciation.

"Okay," she said. "You win. Let's see what's on Netflix." She found an Aubrey Plaza movie and clicked on it. "You like Aubrey, don't you?" she asked Dozer. "She's pretty good."

He didn't answer. He had apparently fallen asleep. She considered moving him off the computer and working, but the movie had started, and it looked interesting. She wasn't married to the idea of working. She just wanted something to distract her from— *No, don't think about her*. The movie would be enough of a distraction. And it was.

Dozer woke up just as the last of the credits rolled across the screen. "Well, damn, buddy. You missed the whole movie." He yawned, stretched, and settled back on the laptop. "I'm afraid you're going to have to move. I need to make myself something to eat."

He made no attempt at leaving, so she gently nudged him off the computer, set the laptop on the coffee table, and went in search of food. He was right there, rubbing on her leg as soon as she opened the refrigerator door. She opened a Tupperware bowl of cooked chicken, smelled it, and gave him a small piece. She knew she was training him to come running every time she opened the fridge, but she didn't care. Or was he training her to give him a treat whenever she got something from the fridge? She wasn't sure. Either way, he won and got what he wanted. She set the container of chicken on the counter and gathered up what she needed to make a sandwich. She was a decent cook but rarely cooked anything just for herself. She'd made wonderful meals for Aliza when they were dating and for the short period of time they'd lived together.

She sighed. Aliza. Sometimes she still missed her. Or maybe she just missed the companionship. She knew she missed having *her person*, someone to do stuff with. She didn't do much with Michael. Now she knew why. He couldn't risk being seen in public with her. "Do I know how to pick 'em or do I know how to pick 'em?" she asked Dozer, who was still rubbing against her legs. "And no, you are not getting more people food. You have plenty of cat food in your dish." She pointed toward it with her chin as if he didn't know where it was. He ignored her, continued his rubbing for a few more seconds, then meandered down the hallway, probably to take another nap on her bed.

She watched another movie while she ate her sandwich, paused it to grab a cookie and a glass of milk, and did her best to keep her thoughts at bay. She was successful—mostly—until she went to bed and Tara made an unexpected but not unwelcome appearance in her dreams.

❖

It was two in the morning when Michael crawled into bed beside Tara. He smelled like beer and stale cigarette smoke. He curled up against her back, and she could tell he was naked, and hard. He stroked her breast and brushed a stubbly cheek against the side of her face. He must have struck out at the bar. There was no way she was going to be his consolation prize. She knew if she pretended to be asleep, he would continue until he woke her up.

"Not tonight," she said. "I've got my period." It was a lie, but she didn't care. He'd lied enough to her lately that she felt justified.

"I don't," he said.

Tara knew him well enough to know that he was asking for oral sex if he couldn't have intercourse with her. The very thought of it made her want to vomit. She'd never liked doing it in the past but complied to keep him happy. There was no way she would ever do that again. Not now that his dick had been in God knows how many other women. "I've got a migraine," Tara said.

"I don't," he repeated.

"Then you can take care of yourself." She didn't care if it sounded harsh. She was not about to give in to him.

He got out of bed, throwing the blankets so that Tara's back was uncovered, and left the room. She pulled the blankets back around her and tried to settle back to sleep. She could hear the muffled sounds of moaning coming from the living room and surmised that he was watching porn on his phone while he *took care of himself.*

She got up and shut the bedroom door to block out the sound. She briefly considered locking it but decided against it. It was one thing to refuse sex; it was another to refuse to let him into the bedroom. That would cause nothing but trouble, and she didn't want to start anything. Not yet, anyway.

CHAPTER FIVE

Tara greeted each child as they came into her classroom. She had a sign on the door with various picture gestures that each child got to pick as they came in. They could choose a hug, a handshake, a high five, or a fist bump from her. Most children chose the hug.

"Miss Foreman," Heather McDonald said as she handed Tara a piece of paper. "I drew you a picture."

"Oh, it's lovely, Heather. I'll hang it on the bulletin board so everyone can admire it."

The girl beamed with pride. She chose to get a hug and then scurried into the classroom to meet up with her friends.

Michael was gone by the time Tara got up for work. And she was glad of it. She vaguely remembered him coming to bed, but he stayed on his own side the rest of the night. She needed to figure out a way to act normal around him, at least until he was served with divorce papers. She didn't know if she had to move out of the house first or if she could do it while still living there and maybe get him to move out until she could find someplace else to live. Moving back to her parents' house was out of the question. Staying with her sister temporarily was a possibility. She needed to talk to her and let her know what was going on anyway. Telling her parents could wait. She didn't need their disapproval at the moment. In fact, she didn't need it at all. Maybe she wouldn't tell them and never see them again. That seemed like a good plan. No more Michael and no more parents.

She looked down when she felt a tug on her sleeve. "Miss Foreman, I picked the hug."

She had been so lost in thought that she hadn't seen Steven come in. "I'm so sorry. I must have been daydreaming." She gave him a squeeze and he scampered off. She did a quick head count. Fifteen. Everyone was present and accounted for. She shut the classroom door and clapped her hands. "Seats, everyone."

Without hesitation, most of the children made their way to their assigned tables and sat down. Two children remained at the back of the classroom, chatting away, oblivious to the fact that their teacher had spoken. "Judith, Kelly, care to join us?" Her words were gentle and kind. She rarely felt the need to raise her voice with this group of kids. She did have some rather rambunctious kids in the past, but this year she seemed to have a group of very cooperative youngsters. She was glad about that, especially today.

"Does anyone have to go potty before we start?" Six hands went up. Three kids put both hands up. "Okay, everyone with your hand up line up at the bathroom door." Ten minutes later, all the children were back at their tables. Several repeated verses of "The Itsy Bitsy Spider" later, Tara passed out cans of Play-Doh so the kids could create their own spiders.

The day seemed to drag by, which was not the usual feeling Tara had working with the children. She called her sister on the way home and made arrangements to meet up with her at her house for dinner. Tara said she would bring the dessert. She stopped at Riverside Bakery and bought a box of vanilla cream puffs, her nephew Brandon's favorite.

Michael wasn't home when Tara pulled into the driveway. She didn't think he would be. He didn't usually get home from work until at least six. Tara sent him a text as soon as she settled in at home. *I'm going to Anna's house for dinner. Do you want me to order you food from Grubhub for supper?*

It took him thirty minutes to respond. *No thanks. I'll just grab something out.*

Another chance to go prowling for a mistress, Tara figured. She was so over it. She didn't care what he did anymore, but she felt sorry for whatever woman he ended up lying to.

She had about an hour and a half to kill before heading to

Anna's, so she sat at the computer in the office and researched divorce lawyers. She was careful to cover her tracks using the incognito mode on the browser. She came up with a list of three possibilities that looked promising. She copied down the information on an index card, folded it in half, and slipped it into her pocket. She could call them the next day before work and make her decision based on their answers.

A half hour later, she was knocking on her sister's door. Anna took forever to answer it. "Sorry," she said. "I was getting Brandon settled. He got a little worked up at school today. Come on in." She stepped back so Tara could walk past her.

"What happened at school?" Tara slipped off her jacket and hung it up on the hook by the door.

"Kids picking on him, and he of course lashes out," Anna answered.

"I thought that's why you put him in private school. To avoid this kind of thing."

Anna headed toward the kitchen with Tara in tow. "That was the plan. Unfortunately, kids can be mean no matter what school they go to." She took several things out of the refrigerator and set them on the counter island.

Tara set the box of cream puffs on the table and sat on a stool across from her. "That's part of why I wanted to talk to you." She watched as Anna ran a head of lettuce under the faucet and set it on a wooden cutting board. "Can I help with anything?" Tara asked.

"Nope. I've got this."

Tara folded her hands. She hesitated to try to find the right words to start the conversation she needed to have. "I'm going to divorce Michael, and I don't know what that means as far as helping you pay for Brandon's school."

In an instant, her sister scooted around the island and wrapped her arms around her. "Oh, honey. I'm so sorry. I know this must be so hard for you."

Tara's parents were the worst, but she was so thankful for her sister. That was the only good thing they had ever given her. "I'm okay. Or I will be. I'm just worried about Brandon and how things might change for him if I can't help."

Anna sat on the stool next to Tara and held her hand. "You

need to do what you need to do for *you*. Not for *us*. Tara, you have never put yourself first. You need to start doing that. Tell me what happened. Why are you and Michael breaking up?"

"First, Michael doesn't know yet. I'm still trying to figure things out. As you know, our prenup says I get a million dollars if he cheats. And he did. Probably a lot."

"How do you know? Do you have proof?"

"I have more than proof. I have his mistress."

Anna stood. "Like locked up somewhere? What do you mean you have her?"

Tara laughed and then laughed some more.

"What?" Anna asked. "Are you okay?"

Tara finally got it under control. "No, I don't have her locked up. I called her and then met with her, and she agreed to help me prove he was cheating with her."

"Wait. You met with the woman he was sleeping with?"

Tara nodded.

"The slut."

Tara shook her head. "No. Not at all. She didn't know he was married, and she broke up with him as soon as she did. She said she would help me."

Anna pulled the cutting board toward herself and proceeded to cut the lettuce into pieces. "And you believe her?"

"Didn't Mom always tell you to gently rip the lettuce and never use a knife?" Tara tipped her chin toward the cutting board.

"Yes. And that's exactly why I do it. Now answer the question. Why do you think this woman should be trusted?"

"I could just tell. I think it was something in her eyes." She did have beautiful eyes.

"Wait. Why were you looking in her eyes? You need to back up here…" She waved the knife in circles, seemingly for emphasis. "Start over. How did you know Michael was sleeping with her? Tell me everything and don't leave anything out." She took a step back, held up one finger, and said, "Hang on. Let me check on Brandon. Don't start without me." She took off down the hallway. When she came back, Tara told her everything.

"And if I had met her any other way, I could see us becoming good friends," Tara said as she finished.

Anna put the chopped lettuce into a bowl and moved on to chopping tomatoes. "Unbelievable."

"I know. I couldn't ask for a better ally. I did some research on divorce lawyers earlier. I am still trying to figure out the questions I should ask—other than their fees."

"What have you got so far?" Anna asked.

"What are your fees?" Tara answered.

"That's it?"

"That's it. See why I need help?"

Brandon came into the room, his head hung down, only looking up briefly at Tara.

"Hey, kiddo," Tara said. "How are you doing?"

"Okay," he answered without looking at her. "Mom, I'm done with my show. I can't get the Xbox to work. Can you help me?"

"Sure," Anna answered. She wiped her hands on a dish towel and followed him into the family room.

Tara swiped a tomato chunk from the cutting board while she waited for Anna.

"So," Anna said when she came back. "Questions for the lawyers. Maybe ask about their experience with prenups." She tapped her chin. "Hmm. What else? How long have you been practicing? Do you actually go to court or are all your cases settled out of court?"

"Oh, those are good. Wait, let me put them in my notes on my phone." She typed away as her sister rattled off questions to ask. "Thank you," she said. "I have just been shaken by this and not thinking as clearly as I should be. But I want to talk to you about Brandon's school costs."

Anna pulled a package of chicken fingers out of the freezer and lined them up on a cookie sheet. "For Brandon," Anna said. "We are having chicken breasts. They're already in the oven."

Tara held up her hands. "I didn't ask. I would be fine if you wanted to feed me chicken nuggets."

"Chicken fingers," Anna corrected her. "You don't even want to know what part of the chicken are considered their nuggets."

Tara laughed. "I love you. You know that?"

"Of course you do. What's not to love?" Anna put her hands in the air and did a little twirl.

"Time to talk turkey, though. No more chicken talk. About Brandon's school?" She raised her eyebrows waiting for some sort of response.

"Tara, if you can't help pay for it anymore, then we will figure something out. I am so appreciative of what you've done so far. You don't owe us anything. You need to take care of yourself now."

Tara found herself tearing up. "I want to be able to help. You're my little sister, and it's my job to take care of you."

"You protected me from Mom and Dad when we were kids. We aren't kids anymore. I'm thirty-four years old. You don't have to take care of me anymore." She handed Tara a napkin. "Wipe the tears that are about to spill out of your eyes and get these crazy thoughts out of your mind. If you win your case and end up loaded, I will be more than happy to take your money. If not, and I put Brandon back in public school, we will survive."

Tara dabbed at the corner of her eyes but didn't respond. She really wanted to help her sister out. She'd been through so much with their parents, Brandon being on the spectrum and her husband dying unexpectedly from a heart attack.

"Get yourself out of that shitty marriage and then we will figure things out," Anna said. "Do you hear me?"

Tara nodded, afraid that if she spoke it might open the dam, and she wouldn't be able to hold back the tears.

"Tara, it's all going to work out in the end. What is it I always say?"

"If it hasn't worked out yet, it's not the end."

"I want you to get as much money as you can from Michael. You deserve it. If there is enough to share, then great, I'll take it. If not, then take care of *you*. I don't think I can say it any clearer. We will survive. Should I sing that Gloria Gaynor song you love so much?"

She started. "At first—"

"Please don't," Tara said with a smirk. "I love *you*. Your singing, not so much."

"I would be highly insulted by that if it wasn't true. I am a terrible singer. Even Brandon tells me to stop."

"Thank you," Tara said.

"There is nothing to thank me for. Call the lawyers. Set

something up. Meet with your new best friend again. What's her name?"

"Megan."

"Meet with Megan. Work out a strategy and get the ball rolling."

The only thing Tara was looking forward to on that list was meeting with Megan again.

Chapter Six

A nd that wraps it up for today," Megan said into the microphone. "Join us next week when our topic will be *can you really make money on YouTube.*"

"Good job," Lynn, their producer, told Megan and Victoria. "I'll go over your research for your next podcast and send you my notes by noon tomorrow."

"Thanks," Victoria said. "I've got a few other ideas too. I'll email them to you."

"Great," Lynn said. "See you in a few days." She packed up her show notes and headed out the door.

"What's going on with you lately?" Victoria asked Megan. "You seem—I don't know—a little off."

"Oh shit. Did I mess up today's show?"

Victoria shook her head. Her long red hair barely moved with the amount of hairspray she must have had in it. "Not at all. But I know you well enough to know something is going on."

Megan took off her headset and leaned back in her chair. "I found out Mike's married." *To a beautiful woman.*

"Well damn. No wonder you're bummed. How did you find out?"

Megan told her about the late-night phone call and then meeting Tara. "And here's the funny part…"

"There's something funny about all this?" Victoria asked.

"I really like her."

"You like the wife of the guy you were sleeping with?"

"I know. I know. But I like her more than I liked him." Megan laughed. "If only I'd met her first."

"Then what?" Victoria asked. "Would you have asked her out?"

Megan stood and grabbed her coat from the back of the chair. "No. That would be a moot point. She's married—to a guy. I don't think she would have been into it. I guess I would have just liked to have her as a friend." She would have to settle for that—if that was even possible.

"So? You've dated guys. Her guy, in fact. And you are into the chicks as well. Maybe she is too."

Megan laughed. "Wouldn't that be a hoot? Going out with my boyfriend's wife?" She slipped her arms into her coat and zipped it up. "I've got to get going. If I'm not home on time, Dozer gets pissed at me. Are you heading out?"

"Yeah. I'm gonna write up a few notes, then I'm heading home. My cat doesn't care how late I stay out."

"You don't even have a cat."

"Good point. But my husband and kid don't seem to get mad at me for being late," Victoria said.

"I'm outta here. Have a good evening."

She waved as she walked out the door, closing it behind her.

At home, she fed Dozer, made herself supper from a can of soup—it was mediocre—and did a load of laundry. She was just settling down on the couch when her phone rang. A quick glance at the caller ID told her it was Tara. She smiled and then literally wiped it off her face with her hand.

"Hello."

"Megan?"

"Yes. Hi, Tara, how are you?"

"I'm hanging in there. You?"

"I'm doing good."

"I found a lawyer. He said he needs to meet with me alone but wanted to talk to you after. Is there any chance you could go with me? Um, you know, to get all the facts straight. I made an appointment for Thursday. I didn't know your work schedule," Tara said. "If Thursday doesn't work for you, I can reschedule."

"I can do Thursday," Megan said. "What time and where?"

"You're easy."

Megan briefly considered saying, *yeah, Michael thought so*, but decided the joke would be in poor taste. "Don't let it get around," she said instead.

There was silence on the other end of the phone and Megan figured that Tara didn't know how to respond. "What time?" she repeated, trying to let Tara off the hook.

"Um. Four o'clock, it's in the building on the corner of Timbolt and Craig Street, Room 107. Do you know where that is?"

"I do. That's across the street from my favorite restaurant."

"Oh," Tara said. "What's the name of it? I don't think I've ever been there."

"Momma's Place. I mean it's not my momma's place." Megan laughed at herself for saying such a stupid thing. "That's the name of it, Momma's Place. Do you like Italian food?"

"I do."

"Maybe I can treat you to dinner after the meeting—I mean if you don't think that's too weird." Of course she would think it's weird.

"We can do that. I'll use any excuse not to go home these days. I'm trying to avoid Michael as much as possible without him getting suspicious. Of course, he's not home much these days. I mean, with his real job, his fake airline job, his fake sick mother, and God knows how many women, he keeps himself pretty busy." She hesitated. "I'm sorry. I shouldn't have said that about all the women."

Megan shook her head even though she knew Tara couldn't see her. "No. It's alright. I've come to grips with the fact that he was using me and I'm probably not the only one. So, Thursday at four and then dinner afterward."

"Yes. But I'm not going to let you pay for me. You are doing me a huge favor. This will be my treat."

The treat will be spending time with you, Megan thought, but didn't dare say. "Hey. You bought me a bottle of water and half a brownie already. I think we are even."

"Not by a long shot. No arguing. I'll see you on Thursday."

"Um. Yes, you will."

They said their good-byes and Megan hung up the phone. She felt almost—what was it? Giddy? Was that right? That was downright strange. And wrong. She tried to shake off the feeling, but it persisted. "What the hell is wrong with me?" she asked Dozer, who was lounging next to her. He didn't answer her. "You're right. There is nothing wrong with me. It's okay to look forward to having dinner with a new friend. Even if we did meet under really weird circumstances. Really weird."

Dozer yawned and stretched.

"You don't really care, do you? Just for that, I'm going to watch what I want to tonight." She grabbed the remote from the coffee table, propped up her feet, and scrolled through Netflix. When nothing caught her attention, she thought Facebook might be a better way to get her mind off Tara. There was a meme with a quote about all great deeds and thoughts having a ridiculous beginning. Megan couldn't help but laugh. She thought it fit her current circumstances perfectly.

Tara's stomach did a rumba and the quickstep as she approached the lawyer's door. Maybe she should stop watching *Dancing with the Stars* before bed. Her nerves settled down as soon as she saw Megan coming up beside her. "Hi," she said shyly. "Thank you so much for coming." She reached for Megan's hand and gave it a squeeze. She felt the warmth radiating off it and wanted to hang on. She reluctantly dropped it and put her hand in her pocket.

"No problem. I'm glad to help."

A secretary announced their arrival, and it only took a few seconds for the lawyer to greet them. "Jackson O'Brian." He offered a hand to each of them in turn.

"I'm Tara Foreman, and this is Megan…" She realized she didn't know Megan's last name.

"Megan Montgomery," Megan said.

"Nice to meet you both. Tara, come on into my office. Megan, you can have a seat, and I'll take your statement in a bit." He stepped back and put his arm out. Tara entered as Megan took a seat in the waiting area. Tara sat across from the desk, and Mr. O'Brian sat in the comfortable-looking leather chair behind it.

The framed documents and diplomas on the wall behind him

looked impressive—and expensive. Tara was sure this was going to cost a whole lot of money. He told her the cost of this initial visit and drawing up divorce papers. The rest would depend on the prenup settlement. She slid a check across the desk tucked away in an envelope. It hurt to give up that much money, but it would hurt more to stay with Michael.

"Thanks," Mr. O'Brian said. "Did you bring a copy of your prenup?"

Tara handed him a manila envelope with the document that she and Michael had signed two weeks before they got married.

He took a few minutes to look it over.

Tara glanced at Megan. Megan gave her a reassuring smile. It helped. "Well? What do you think, Mr. O'Brian?" Tara asked when he finished and set the document on his desk.

"You have a solid case here, provided we can prove the infidelity. And please call me Jackson."

"That is where Megan comes in. She's my proof."

"Yes. You said that on the phone." Jackson pressed a button on his intercom and asked his secretary to send Megan in. She took a seat next to Tara, and Jackson turned his attention to her. "Can you tell me how you met Mr. Foreman?"

Megan cleared her throat. "It was at the Happy Hour Bar on Monroe Ave. I…I…um, don't usually hang out in bars or meet men that way."

Jackson smiled and put his hands up. "No judgment here. Just looking for the facts." From his desk drawer he pulled a yellow legal pad—how appropriate—and took notes. "Go on. When was this? Who approached who? And so on?"

Megan filled him in on the details of their first meeting. Tara listened with interest how her husband had approached her, struck up a conversation and then a relationship. She was surprised that it only made her a little sick to her stomach. She'd thought finding out the details might make her throw up. Of course, they hadn't gotten to any intimate details yet.

"And I know this is delicate," Jackson said. "But when was the first time you slept together, who initiated it, and where did it take place?"

And there it was.

Megan looked over at Tara before beginning. "I'm sorry," she said. And Tara could tell that she meant it.

Megan turned her attention back to Jackson. Tara tried to block out the words she was saying, but it was no use. She might not love Michael, but his betrayal still hurt.

Megan apologized again when she was done—or thought she was done.

"I hate to ask, but I need a little more information." He proceeded to ask some very direct, very personal questions. "Very good," he said when he finished with Megan. "And I need to talk to Tara again for a moment, please." He escorted her to the door of his office and then returned to Tara.

"I'm going to need your financial documents, bank records, insurance documents, pay stubs, and such. I'll email you the exact list. Speaking of which, does your husband have your passwords, or do you share an email address?"

"No. He rarely uses the computer."

"Good. I'll make copies of your documents, and you keep the originals. Make sure they are in a secure place and your husband doesn't have access to them." He told her several more things she needed to do and consider. He asked what seemed like a thousand questions. "I know this is overwhelming. It will all be in the email. I'm assuming you want to move ahead with this?"

"Absolutely."

"Very good," he repeated. He pulled two business cards from his desk drawer and handed them to Tara before he stood up, walked to the door, and opened it. "One for you and one for Megan. Have a good day, Tara. I'll be in touch."

Megan stood up as Tara went back into the waiting area, and they walked together silently down the hall.

"Are you okay?" Megan asked when they got to the door leading outside. Tara shook her head, afraid that if she spoke, she would start crying. That was the last thing she wanted to do, especially in front of Megan. She'd done enough crying during the months leading up to this—when she suspected Michael of cheating but had no proof. She wanted that part to be done. She didn't want to hurt over him anymore.

The hug Megan pulled her into was a surprise. A welcome one.

A comforting one. A—she wasn't sure. Her heart started pounding in her chest. She pulled back, afraid Megan would feel it too.

"I'm…I'm so sorry," Megan said. "I didn't mean to—"

"No. It's fine. I'm fine. I'm the one who's sorry. You are doing so much to help me, and I really appreciate it." She willed the beating in her chest to slow down. She cleared her throat. "I'm still up for dinner if you are." The last thing she wanted to do was go home, and spending more time with Megan would be nice. Crazy. This was just crazy. "The food better be as good as you said it is," she teased her, trying to lighten the mood.

Megan grimaced. "Oh man. I hope it is too. I don't want you to be disappointed or pissed at me." She opened the glass door leading out of the building and motioned for Tara to go first. "Tell you what. If it sucks, I promise I'll make you a homemade meal to make up for it."

"Oh yeah. You cook?" They started toward the crosswalk.

"I cook. Not often. But I cook."

"Like frozen pizza?" Tara raised her eyebrows.

"Hey. I'll have you know that I make the best frozen pizza this side of the Mississippi."

"And who makes the best frozen pizza on the other side of the Mississippi?" Tara waited for the walk sign to change and then started across the street with Megan by her side.

"I don't know. I've never been to the other side of the Mississippi."

Tara stopped walking when they reached the sidewalk on the other side. "You've never been to the other side? Seriously?"

Megan took two more steps before she must have realized that Tara had stopped. "What?"

"You haven't done much traveling?"

"Not much," Megan replied. "I've been to Canada to visit relatives when I was younger. Other than that, I haven't been out of New York State. Why? Have you traveled a lot?"

"It was one of the perks of being married to a man with money. He likes to spend it, and traveling was one of his favorite things to do."

Megan pulled the zipper up higher on her jacket and wrapped her arms around herself.

Tara hadn't realized how cold it had gotten. "Let's go inside before we freeze to death."

They made their way into the restaurant. It was still early for the dinner rush, so they got a table right away.

The waiter handed them both a menu and said he would be back to take their drink orders. Tara took a quick look at the alcoholic beverage list.

"I've always wanted to see the world," Megan said. "Just didn't have it in my budget. We did go to Niagara Falls when we were kids."

Tara laughed. "With all the traveling we have done, I've never been there. It's practically in our backyard."

"Your backyard must be huge," Megan said. " 'Cause it took us over an hour to get there."

Tara laughed again. She never imagined she'd be laughing so soon after meeting with the lawyer and listening to all the sordid details he had to drag out of Megan. "It's big, but not that big." She felt a rush of sadness at the realization that she would be losing that yard soon. She had spent so much time there, planting flowers and even an apple tree. She spent four days deciding on a patio set for the deck and loved to have her morning cup of coffee there in the summer. There was so much she would be giving up in order to gain her freedom.

"What's going on?" Megan must have sensed the shift in her mood.

"I just realized that at some point I'm going to lose that."

"The yard? Can't you fight to keep your house?"

"Michael owned the house when we got married. I don't think I would stand a chance of getting it. I probably should have asked the lawyer about that."

"If you win this, you'll have enough money to buy your own house with whatever kind of yard you want." She paused and seemed to be studying Tara. "I mean, I know it's not the same, but it will be yours. All yours."

"Thank you."

"For what?"

"For saying that. I forget sometimes that there is a future after this. I've kind of been thinking that the divorce is the end."

"Oh, no," Megan said. "It's just the beginning. You can do anything. Go anywhere. Live anywhere. See whoever you want to."

See whoever I want? Tara hadn't thought about that. She had all but cut her parents out of her life. She no longer cared what they thought. She could start dating women. Oh my God! She could start dating women.

"And now you're smiling," Megan said.

They were interrupted by the waiter. "Can I get you ladies something to drink?"

"Get anything you like," Tara said to Megan. "Remember, it's my treat."

"I'll just get water," Megan said.

"Are you sure?" Tara asked her. "I'm going to get wine. I can get a bottle, if you'll share it with me."

Megan smiled. It lit up her face and those dimples appeared. Those delicious dimples. Stop, Tara ordered her brain. You start thinking about dating women and suddenly they all look good to you.

"Okay," Megan responded. "It's good to share. I learned that in kindergarten."

"Excellent." Tara turned to the waiter. "A bottle of Tyrrell's Hunter Valley Semillion, please."

"Very good, ma'am." He turned and left.

"It's from Australia," Tara said to Megan. "We'll get you to see the world yet."

"Have you been to Australia?" Megan asked.

"I'm almost embarrassed to say yes."

"Why?"

"I feel like I'm bragging or something. I don't know. It's not like I was the one that paid for it."

"You shouldn't feel embarrassed about that. I certainly would have gone given the chance."

"You said you went to Niagara Falls when you were a kid. Who did you go with? I really don't know much about you."

"My parents and my sister," Megan replied. "I think I was ten."

"Is your sister older or younger than you?" *And where did you get those dimples? STOP IT, brain. Or is it my libido, just because I have an attractive woman in front of me?*

"Three years younger. She is married with a baby. Harper is eleven months old."

"Oh, I love that name. I have a sister too. She's a couple years younger than me. And what about your parents?" Tara found she really did want to get to know Megan better.

"They're both older than me."

Tara laughed. Again. "I figured that much. Are they still alive?"

"My dad is. My mom died a year and a half ago."

"I'm so sorry. Were you close?"

Megan nodded. "We were. I'm still close to my sister and dad. I see them often."

The waiter returned with the bottle of wine. He uncorked it, poured a small amount into Tara's glass, and handed it to her. She sipped it, swirled it around her mouth, and let it coat her tongue. It was something Michael had taught her years ago. She nodded her approval to the waiter. He poured more wine into her glass and then poured some into Megan's.

"Are you ready to order?" he asked.

"I'm sorry," Tara said. "We haven't even looked at the menus. Can we have a few minutes?"

"Of course." He made his way to the next table, order pad in hand.

Megan picked up her menu and peered over the top of it. "How about your parents?"

"Also older than me. And still alive. Unfortunately."

Megan put the menu down. "Unfortunately?"

"I probably shouldn't have said that. They weren't the best parents. Still aren't. They were basically the reason I married Michael."

"What does that mean?"

Tara took a deep breath to give herself time to figure out how to answer. "Part of it was them pushing me to marry him and part of it was me wanting to get away from them." She wasn't sure she wanted to get into more details. She was relieved when Megan didn't ask for any.

"Wow. I'm so sorry. That sucks."

"It does, but I'm the one that let them push me around. I'm

done with that. No one is going to do that to me again." She picked up her menu. "Do you know what you're going to get?"

"I've never had a bad meal here. Sooo..." She dragged the word out. "I don't know."

"That—is not helpful."

"Okay. I'll decide. Then I'll force you to get what I'm getting."

Tara was momentarily confused. "Oh. You're trying to push me around. Right?"

Megan laughed. "Just testing you. I would never actually push you around. I'm a live and let live kind of gal."

"I like that," Tara said. And I like you."

Megan folded her menu and set it on the table. "I'm going to get the sirloin steak tips."

"Hmm. Believe it or not, I was leaning that way too."

I wish you would lean my way, Megan thought. It wasn't the first time she'd had feelings for a straight woman. But having feelings for Tara was just plain stupid considering the circumstances that they met under. "Good choice."

"I thought so. Tell me more about your family. How did your mother die?"

"She had a stroke. Very unexpected." It still hurt to think about it, but Megan rarely cried over the loss anymore. "The funny thing is she was always so active and health conscious. I tend to be the opposite. It's not that I mind going for a hike or playing tackle football, but I tend to be more of a couch potato, and I will fight to the death for my right to eat a donut."

"Tackle football?"

"I threw that in to see if you were listening." The smile that covered Tara's face was worth the silly joke. "Actually, I played tackle football when I was a kid with the neighborhood boys. They eventually banned me for being too rough. I was never afraid to throw my whole body into knocking them down. I even made Stanley Barns cry. I think we were nine years old at the time."

"Were you a bully?"

"Not at all. I was just very competitive. I helped Stanley up and walked him home. I didn't even tell his mother that he was tackled by a girl. See, I cared."

"Tell me about your mom."

The request surprised Megan. Most people avoided the subject since she'd lost her mother, and usually changed the subject when Megan brought her up. It was as if they thought that if they didn't talk about it, it wouldn't hurt so bad. "She was the best. Always stopped what she was doing if I needed her attention. She told the corniest jokes and would laugh her head off halfway through so that she had trouble finishing it. I would laugh more at her laughing than at the joke itself. I never doubted that she loved me or my sister. She and my dad met when they were in seventh grade and had been together ever since."

"She sounds wonderful."

"She was. Your mom, not so much, huh?"

"No. Not at all. If I had to sum her up in one word, I would say she was a mean fucker. Pardon my French." She sipped her wine.

"Um, I think that is more than one word, and it didn't sound French to me. I believe it would be *méchant connard.*"

"For real? You speak French?"

"I took it in high school. I can count to ten and swear. That's about it. I'm not a hundred percent sure what I said is right, so don't go quoting me."

"Never."

The waiter approached the table. "Have we decided, or do you need more time?"

"All set," Megan said. She gave her order and waited while Tara gave hers, collected both menus, and handed them to him.

"Very good," the waiter said and was gone.

"So," Megan said. "Not the best childhood?"

"No. I had my sister on my team. For some reason my parents weren't as hard on her as on me, but when they were, I did my best to protect her."

"You mentioned that she has a son with autism?"

"Brandon. Yes. He's thirteen. He can be a handful. I'm not sure how she does it. Her husband died, so she's a single parent."

Megan listened as Tara told her about her sister and nephew and their struggles. It wasn't long before their food arrived. They continued talking between bites. The food, as usual, didn't disappoint. Neither did the wine. Tara had made a wonderful choice.

Megan objected to Tara paying when the bill arrived, but Tara won the argument.

"Thanks so much for the meal," Megan said as they walked back to their cars. "I really appreciate it."

"You're the one doing me the favor. I really appreciate you. Here's my car," Tara said. "I also appreciate your company and support. I can't tell you how much it means to me."

Megan had the urge to hug her but resisted. "It's no problem. I'm happy to help." And she meant it. Sure, Mike had done Megan wrong, but he had really been a shithead when it came to Tara. Helping her was the least she could do.

Tara unlocked her car door with her key fob but seemed to hesitate before getting in. "Can I call you sometime?" she asked. A blush creeped up her neck. "I mean, you understand the situation. I haven't told anyone else except for my best friend and sister. They are very supportive but have never been through anything like this."

Megan was touched and happy that Tara had asked. "Of course. I would like that very much." Very much. She again had the urge to hug Tara. She took a step back to make sure she didn't act on the urge. "Well, drive careful. Call whenever you would like."

"That goes both ways," Tara said. "You feel free to call too." She got into her car and Megan stood on the sidewalk, watching her until she drove away.

"There goes trouble," she said out loud to no one. "I need to get ahold of my emotions or I'm the one that is going to be in trouble."

CHAPTER SEVEN

I t went well," Tara said to Cori after work.

Cori set a glass of wine on the end table next to Tara and sat in the chair across from her. "So, you're happy with this lawyer?"

"So far, so good. Of course we're just at the beginning of the process, but he seemed to be asking all the right questions."

"And Michael? Do you think he suspects anything?" She pushed the plate of cheese and crackers on the coffee table between them closer to Tara.

"Not that I can tell. Of course I can't really read him anymore. I probably never could and just didn't realize it."

"He puts on a good act. He had me fooled," Cori said. "I thought he was a good guy."

"Yeah. He still acts like a good guy," Tara said, using air quotes, "when other people are around. When it's just him and me, he pretty much ignores me. Unless of course he wants sex. I can't even imagine giving in to that with him anymore. He's been pushing for it lately, which tells me he hasn't replaced Megan yet."

"On that subject, tell me about her. You said you had dinner after the meeting with the lawyer? I have to say I'm surprised. I would think you wouldn't want anything to do with her."

Tara thought back on the time she'd spent with Megan and had to consciously control a smile. "I did. And she's actually very nice. She didn't have to agree to help me, and she stepped right up anyway."

"What aren't you telling me?" Cori asked.

Tara knew that Cori could almost read her mind sometimes. "What do you mean?" She knew exactly what Cori meant.

"There's something else going on in that little brain of yours. I just can't tell if it's something about Michael or the lawyer." She paused. "No. I think it's something about Megan. At first, I thought maybe you were liking your lawyer a little too much. But now I think you like Megan."

"What?" Tara sipped her wine as she tried to keep any readable expression from her face.

"Don't what me. I know you, and I know when you're keeping something from me. Spill."

Tara glanced up at the ceiling, trying to get her thoughts in order. If there was anyone in this world she could tell her feelings to, it was Cori.

"Tara."

Tara brought her eyes to Cori's, then looked away. It would be easier to *spill*, as Cori put it, without looking at her. "I like her."

"You like her, or you *like* her?"

"I like her. I know that's weird considering everything. I can see what Michael saw in her. I know, I know. That sounds so sick." She brought her eyes back to Cori's. "And she mentioned that she has an ex-girlfriend. So, I know she's bi or pan or whatever label everyone is using these days."

"Are you sure she wasn't just talking about a friend? I know people that use the word 'girlfriend' as just a friend."

Tara shook her head. "She said the ex-girlfriend had cheated on her. I don't think she would have said it like that if she had just been a friend."

Cori took a long swig of her wine and seemed to be mulling over the information Tara had just given her. "Do you plan on acting on your feelings?"

"Are you crazy? Of course not. The woman slept with my husband."

"But she didn't know he was married, you said. So she is innocent in all this."

"Yeah, but it would still be weird—and wrong." And oh, so delicious.

"Can we talk about your feelings for women?" Cori asked. "We've never really talked about it after you told me. I got the feeling you wanted to bury it, so I never brought it up."

Tara stuffed a cracker topped with a piece of Swiss cheese into her mouth, giving her time to think. She did need to talk to someone about it, and Cori was obviously the best and safest choice. She nodded.

"You told me you had feelings, but you never used the word 'gay.' Would you consider yourself that? Gay, I mean? Or are you bi? You're obviously married to a man and have had sex with him. Have you ever had sex with a woman? And was Michael the only guy you ever had sex with?"

"Wow," Tara said. "Have you been storing up the questions?"

"I've been wondering," Cori answered honestly. "But I didn't think I should ask."

"You can ask me anything, Cori. The answer is no to having sex with other men or with any woman."

"Then how do you know you like women?"

It was a reasonable question and one that Tara had asked herself many times. The answer was always the same. "Because when I think about being with a woman, my body reacts. You know what I mean. The thought of kissing a woman turns me on way more than full-on sex with Michael."

"And you're sure that it's just not that Michael isn't good in bed?"

Tara laughed. "He's not bad in bed. I think Megan would agree with that." The thought of Megan and Michael made her sick to her stomach. But it wasn't Michael she realized she was sick over. It was the thought of Megan with someone else. This was so wrong, and she knew it. But she couldn't help it. "I don't know how else to explain it. I've always been drawn to women. I just never acted on it because of the brainwashing my parents did."

"So, you would consider yourself gay, then?"

"Without a doubt. One of the positive things about divorcing Michael is the freedom to finally be myself. Just the thought of that feels like a weight has been lifted off me. Catching Michael cheating is actually a blessing. I never thought I would feel that way, but I do."

"If I ever caught Marcus cheating, I'd have to go full Lorena Bobbitt on him."

"I don't think you have anything to worry about. That man thinks you hung the moon," Tara said. She took another sip of her wine. Time with Cori was just what she needed, and the fact that she could be totally honest with her was something she never took for granted.

"As well he should."

"What else do you want to know?"

"You know Megan likes girls. You like girls. What would stop you from pursuing her?"

The reaction that Tara's body had at the thought was both shocking and exhilarating. "For one thing, I'm still married. If I cheat, I get nothing. For another, I can't go after my husband's girlfriend. Not to mention the fact that I have never pursued a woman in my life. I wouldn't have any idea how to even do that."

"I would think it's the same way you pursue a man—only nicer."

"You seem to forget that I've never done that either. Michael is the one that came after me. I never would have chased him. I never would have even been interested in him if it wasn't for my parents. My experience with either gender is pretty much nothing."

"How about online dating?"

"I've heard so many horror stories about that." Could she do that? Go online and meet a stranger? "Men pretending to be women and such."

"That's why you don't meet anyone without talking to them on the phone first. At least that would reassure you." Cori piled a piece of cheese onto a cracker and topped it off with another cracker.

"Let's go back to the fact that I'm still married."

Cori covered her mouth, finished chewing her food, and said, "Oh yeah, there is that."

"Anything like that needs to wait. I've waited this long. I can wait a little longer."

"Did the lawyer say how long to expect this to take?"

"He said it would depend on whether Michael wanted to fight this or not. I really pray he doesn't. But if he does, I'm not going to back down. I deserve that money, and I really want to continue to help my sister pay for Brandon's school. She said not to worry about it, but I do. I know it would be a major burden if I can't help."

"I hate to say it, but she's right. You need to look out for you."

Tara put her hands up. "Please don't. I *want* to help her. I feel like I *need* to help her."

"Okay. I won't argue the point. The plan is to get Megan's testimony, divorce Michael, get a huge settlement, help your sister, find a beautiful woman, and live happily ever after."

"That's the plan." Tara sent a silent prayer to God or the Universe or whoever was listening that it would work out that way.

The trailer for the new movie that played during the commercial break was one Megan had been waiting for. Sandra Bullock was her favorite actress, and she never failed to entertain. She hated going to the theater alone, and Jill wasn't available for such adventures since Harper was born. Megan didn't hold that against her. Jill had wanted a child since she was small. Megan was happy for her. There were several friends she considered before Tara came to mind. Tara. Megan liked her. Really liked her. She needed to stop that. No, she shouldn't be inviting her to the movies. No. She shouldn't.

Hi. Any interest in seeing a movie with me Friday evening? She hit send and her text traveled through the ether to Tara.

Sure. Time? Where should I meet you? Tara didn't even ask what the movie was.

Seven thirty, Movie Time on Turner Road. Meet you in the lobby? Megan texted.

Wonderful. See you there.

"I went and done did it now. Didn't I?" She willed her heart—or was it something located lower in her body—to calm down. No. This was okay. She could handle her attraction. It wasn't as if she hadn't had crushes in the past. This one somehow felt different. Maybe because she was Mike's wife. No. She didn't think that was it. He was out of the picture. Megan's focus had rapidly changed from him to her. And she liked *her* so much better.

Megan had a couple of days to come to her senses and cancel their plans, but as the two days passed, she was looking more and more forward to seeing Tara. She arrived at the theater twenty minutes early, bought two tickets, and settled on the padded benches by the game room. She could easily see the front door from her vantage point.

A woman walked in with light brown hair, wearing a coat similar to the one Tara had worn the couple of times Megan had seen her. Megan jumped to her feet as her heart leaped in her chest, only to realize it wasn't Tara. She silently reprimanded herself for getting so excited.

When she did spot Tara walking in, she managed to control herself and rose slowly instead of jumping up. She wasn't so successful at controlling the reaction of her heart.

Tara turned her way, and Megan waved her over. "Hi," she said.

"Hi, yourself. I'm so glad you asked me to join you. I haven't been out to the movies in ages. It's too easy to stay home nowadays and just stream one. But there's nothing like seeing it on the big screen." She smiled that beautiful smile.

"I agree. Thanks for coming." Megan held up the tickets. "Shall we?"

"Let me pay you for my ticket," Tara said.

"Absolutely not. My treat. I believe…" She looked at the top ticket. "We need to go to seven." There were a total of ten theaters, each showing a different movie.

"Lead the way." Tara followed. They got there just as the lights were going down and the previews were starting.

It took a few moments for Tara's eyes to adjust to the darkness and Megan was several steps ahead of her by the time they did. The small lights on the floor at the edge of the seats helped. From this distance, even in the dim light, she had the perfect view of Megan's rear end. She took a few moments to study it, decide it was perfect, and then squash the urge to grab it. Not that she could have with the distance that was rapidly increasing between them. She hurried to catch up. She reached her just as Megan turned.

"Are these seats okay?" Megan asked. "I don't like to sit too close."

"Perfect." *Just like that cute butt you've got there.* What was it about Megan that drew her in? It was nothing and everything all at the same time. How was that even possible?

Megan moved aside and gestured for Tara to go in first. "Oh man. I forgot to ask you if you wanted popcorn or a drink. I can go get it."

"No. I don't want anything. But it won't bother me if you do."

Megan sat. Next to her. Close to her. Which was actually the only option. While the theater had replaced most of the outdated seats in the building, they hadn't replaced these, and they were pretty tight quarters. Not that Tara minded. Actually, she minded that she didn't mind. She liked having Megan this close and she knew she shouldn't. Nothing I can do about it, she thought. I'll have to suffer through it. And suffer though her smelling like vanilla and sandalwood. And her arm brushing against mine. She turned to look at Megan in the glow from the movie screen. She was smiling at whatever they were showing. The light cast a shadow, making her dimples look even deeper. The urge to kiss her startled Tara, and she pulled her eyes away. What was wrong with her? This was the last person she should be lusting after. First of all, she hardly knew her. And second, she was the one Michael had an affair with— well, one of probably many. And there were so many more reasons. Although she couldn't think of any at the moment. She put her libido away and turned her attention to the previews.

She wouldn't think about the woman sitting next to her again. No. Not at all. She was glad to have a new friend. That was it. Nothing more. No sir. No way. Megan brushed against her arm. Shit. Tingles. Why? She put both her hands firmly in her lap and away from Megan's wild arm brushes.

She was still thinking about Megan—despite her brain's objections—when the movie started. It was actually very engaging, and she found herself caught up in it. She had successfully forgotten that Megan was even sitting next to her. Except when she laughed. Or didn't laugh. Or smiled. Or when a stream of tears ran down her cheek at the sad part and she didn't bother to wipe them away. Tara admired her for that. She never let people see her cry. Not since she was five and discovered it gave her parents more power over her.

"I really liked that," Megan whispered, way too close to her ear. "What did you think?"

"It was good."

Megan made no attempt to get up as everyone else rushed out.

The room was empty by the time she rose. "I don't know about you, but I don't feel like going home. Would you like to go get a drink or something to eat? There's lots of places nearby."

No. Yes. *Stop being ridiculous.* "I would."

"Great. Barney's next door? They have food and drinks."

"Sure."

Tara pulled the collar of her coat up higher around her neck against the chilly night air as they walked the short distance to the pub. It wasn't as crowded as it could have been for a Friday night, probably because they didn't have big screen TVs playing various football games like some of the other bars.

They chose a table and ordered drinks. Tara relaxed into their conversation. She chalked up her earlier feelings to the close proximity in which they were seated and her lack of intimacy in recent months. Not that she wanted to be intimate with Michael. But she did miss the closeness of another human being. By the time they said their good nights, she was sure her misplaced feelings toward Megan were just a passing phase. She was glad they'd become friends. She was sure that was all they ever would—could—be. Well, almost sure.

"What are you doing on Saturday?" Tara asked over the phone.

"A quick trip to Paris for a manicure in the morning and then nothing after that," Megan answered.

"Why are you going to Paris when you can only count to ten and swear in French? Shouldn't you be going to some English-speaking country for that? Like, I don't know, New Zealand?"

"I do like their accents. Maybe I'll reconsider. Why? What's going on Saturday? Another meeting with the lawyer?"

"No. Michael is spending the day at his buddy's house playing pool. At least that's what he told me. Doesn't matter. I was thinking that it's time you stepped out of New York State and did a little sightseeing. What would you say to taking a trip to Philadelphia? We could see the Liberty Bell, go to the Museum of Art, pose for pictures on the steps Rocky ran up. What do you say?"

Megan only had to think about it for a second. "Sounds like it would be great."

"Excellent," Tara said. "I can pick you up in the morning, say around seven, if that's not too early for you."

"I usually sleep till noon, but I can make an exception this one time."

"Noon? I mean, you can sleep in the car while I drive, if that would help."

"I'm just kidding," Megan said. "I'm usually up by seven anyway. My cat hates it when I sleep in."

"You have a cat? You'll have to tell me all about him or her on the ride."

"You got it. What do you need me to bring? Anything?"

"Nope. It's just a day trip. We'll probably get back late, but you shouldn't need anything. I'll bring snacks. Is there anything you don't like? I'll make sure I have donuts."

Megan was touched and surprised that Tara had remembered she liked donuts. "I hate sardines."

"I wasn't going to bring sardines anyway. Okay. I'll let you go. See you bright and early Saturday morning. Text me your address when we hang up."

"You got it. I am looking forward to this. Thank you."

"No thanks necessary. I am looking forward to it too. It will be fun. And God knows I could use some fun. See you then. Bye."

"Bye." Megan hung up the phone and turned to Victoria, who had apparently been listening to her conversation.

"Maybe our next podcast should be about dating your boyfriend's wife," Victoria said.

"Ha ha. Aren't you just so funny. It's not a date, and how did you know that was Tara? It could have been my sister." Megan sat in her chair and put her headset around her neck.

"I've never seen you light up like that when you've talked to Jill." Victoria took her seat as well.

Megan looked at her wrist as if she was wearing a watch. "Where's Lynn? She's late."

"Nice deflection. And Lynn's not late. We don't have to talk about it if you don't want to. But your face did light up like the

Fourth of July. If you're not going to be honest with me, at least be honest with yourself. Watch your heart, my friend, with this one."

"There's nothing to watch," Megan said. "There's nothing going on."

"Okay. You keep telling yourself that."

The door opened and Lynn walked in. "Telling yourself what?" she asked.

"Nothing." Megan gave Victoria *a shut up about this* look.

"Whatever," Lynn said. "Are you two ready for today's show?"

"Sure are," Victoria said.

"Anything we need to go over before we start?" Lynn asked.

"I'm set," Victoria said.

"Me too," Megan chimed in.

"Great. Then let's start," Lynn said.

Megan put her headset on and pulled the microphone in front of her closer. Victoria did the same.

Lynn signaled them and Victoria started. "Welcome to another episode of *And Now This*. I'm Victoria Prattle here with Megan Montgomery, and today's topic is a good one. Can you really make money with YouTube?"

"That's right," Megan added. "The place I see the most people claiming you can make money on YouTube is on YouTube itself. Today we are taking a deep dive to see if it's really possible. What are your thoughts, Victoria?"

They spent the next fifty-five minutes discussing the topic before wrapping it up.

"Great show," Lynn said.

"Oh crap," Megan said.

"What?" Lynn asked her.

"Forgot I was supposed to text something to a friend. I was going to do it before the show, but Victoria distracted me." She gave Victoria her best fake mean girl look.

"Hey," Victoria said. "Don't blame me if you're distracted. I'm not the one running barefoot through your mind."

Lynn gave Megan a look. "Distracted by Mike lately?"

"Mike is yesterday's news," Victoria volunteered.

"He is? So, someone new is running naked through Megan's mind?" Lynn teased her.

Megan tried to dislodge the vision of Tara running naked. It didn't work.

"I said barefoot," Victoria corrected her. "Not naked. Although she could be naked in Megan's mind."

"Okay," Megan said. "There is no one running naked or barefoot anywhere." She turned to Lynn. "Yes. I broke up with Mike. It wasn't working out." She liked Lynn but it had always been more of a working relationship than a friendship. She didn't feel the need to fill her in on the details. The look she gave Victoria told her she better not be filling them in either.

Lynn put up her hands. "Sorry. Just teasing. And I am sorry things didn't work out with Mike."

"It's okay. Victoria just has the wrong idea. I've got a few ideas for some upcoming shows if you have time to discuss them."

Lynn looked at her watch. "I've got some time to spare. What did you have in mind?"

"Hang on one sec," Megan said. She sent a quick text to Tara apologizing for the delay and giving her the address and apartment number where she lived. She told her to just text when she got there so she didn't have to climb the flight of stairs to her apartment. Megan was in the middle of her discussion with Lynn when her phone pinged in her pocket announcing that she had an incoming text. She waited—with much difficulty—until she was done talking to Lynn and on the way to her car before reading it.

No problem, and a flight of stairs doesn't scare me. There was a smiling face emoji. Megan was sure her smile matched the little yellow guy's smile. Victoria was right. She did need to watch her heart with this one.

Chapter Eight

The knock on her door told Megan that Tara had arrived. She opened it and grabbed Dozer as he was about to escape. It wasn't the first time he'd wanted to wander the halls, but Megan didn't feel like chasing him down to Mrs. Anderson's place, where he knew he would get a treat. "Hi," she said to Tara as she stood back up, Dozer in her arms.

"Hey there," Tara said to the cat, giving him a scratch on the head. "Hi to you too," she said to Megan. "Who's this little guy?" She stepped in and Megan closed the door behind her.

"This is Dozer," she said.

"Dozer cause he likes to sleep?"

"No," Megan responded. "Dozer cause he likes to plow into things like a bulldozer." She set him on the floor, and he circled her legs, leaning against her. She looked at him. "Don't try to butter me up. I saw you trying to escape." He sauntered off down the hall as if he was mad that his effort to get back into Megan's good graces had failed. "And there he goes," Megan said after him. They heard a crash. "And that is why his name is Dozer. Let me see what he's gotten into, and I'll be right back."

She found the jar of Q-tips that Dozer had knocked over and placed it back on the counter, grateful that it was made of plastic and not glass. "Hey," she said to him. "Go lie down on my bed and stay out of trouble until I get back." He ignored her order and jumped up on the counter again. She scooped him up and deposited him on the bed.

"All set," Megan said when she rejoined Tara. She grabbed her jacket off the hook by the door and followed Tara down to her car.

"Drinks in the cooler in the back." Tara put the car in reverse and pulled out of the parking space. "Snacks in the box next to it. And a dozen fresh donuts in the box directly behind you. Help yourself."

"Whoa," Megan said. "I may never leave this car."

"Well, I didn't bring a potty, so you might have to. Please."

"Please don't potty in your car?" Megan laughed. "Okay. I won't. Scout's honor." She held up her pinkie finger.

Tara glanced at her. "Nope. Still not right. You should probably google Scout's honor to learn how to do that correctly."

"Damn. I thought I had it that time." Megan looked out the window. Light snow was starting to flutter down. "I didn't think it was supposed to snow today."

"One thing you can count on is the weather forecaster being wrong. If any other profession was off as much as they are, they wouldn't last long."

"So true. But I can't imagine it's easy to predict the weather. Even if they get it right in one area, twenty miles away may be very different."

"I like your attitude. You seem to look on the bright side of things." Tara turned on the intermittent windshield wipers.

"I try," Megan replied. "Sometimes it's not easy. Some situations take a lot of time to see the bright side." She turned toward Tara. "I have to say that the bright side of finding out I was dating a married man is making a new friend." She paused. "At least I hope you consider me a friend."

Tara looked at her. "Of course." She turned her attention back to the road. "That is the bright side for me too." She smiled.

The snow continued on the five-hour drive to Philadelphia, and only seemed to come down harder as they approached the city. The conversation was as steady as the snow.

"Here we are," Tara said as she pulled into a parking lot near the Philadelphia Museum of Art. "I'm not sure with this weather if we want to run up the steps to re-create Rocky's famous scene. I can imagine slipping and tumbling down them."

"In that case," Megan said. "I'm okay with skipping it. I would prefer not to see that happen. Maybe you can just pose at the top and I'll take your picture."

Tara found a parking space close to the museum. "How about we both pose, and we'll find someone else to take the picture?"

"Deal." Megan pulled the collar of her coat up once she was out of the car. Not only was it snowing, but it felt at least ten degrees colder than when they'd left that morning. Snow in early November wasn't unusual, but this degree of cold was. "Maybe we should do the picture now before it gets any colder."

They made their way to the building, passing by the statue of Sylvester Stallone as Rocky. There was a crowd of people around it, so they didn't take the path that would bring them closer. Megan paused long enough to take a picture of it with her phone. "Holy shit," she said when they were in front of the museum. "Those are a lot of steps."

"I'm sorry," Tara said. "Maybe I should have parked in the underground garage so we could have bypassed the steps and just taken the elevator up. It's not too late to go back to the car and do that."

"Nope," Megan said. "I'm up for this if you are. I wouldn't have eaten three donuts on the drive if I had realized the workout I would be getting. On the other hand, it's probably a good thing to get a workout after eating three donuts. Let's go." She started toward the steps, thankful for whoever had shoveled them. "I can do this. I can do this."

"You can do this," Tara said, coming up behind her.

Megan was breathless by the time they reached the top landing. "You okay?" Tara asked.

"Yep," Megan managed to squeak out. She bent and put her hands on her legs above her knees. "I just need a minute." Her legs felt numb from the cold and warm from exertion. She wondered how that was even possible.

"Take your time."

"I can't take too much time. We'll freeze to death out here."

She stood up and stomped her feet. She wasn't sure if it was to try to dissipate the numb feeling or the lactic acid that had built up causing the burning sensation. "Ready," she said.

"Wait. I want to get a picture." Tara stopped a couple passing by and asked if they would mind taking their picture. The man took her phone, went back down a few steps, and waited until they posed.

Tara wrapped her arm around Megan's shoulder. The tingle that ran through Megan settled squarely in her center. She took a breath in and held it as she willed the feeling to leave. Not that she really wanted it to, but she knew it could only lead to frustration.

"Thank you," Tara told the man when he handed her phone back to her. "Let's get you inside," she said to Megan. "Don't want you freezing to death. I would hate to have to call your family and tell them I killed you."

"Lead the way."

Despite Megan's argument, Tara paid for both of their tickets.

"Oh my God," Megan said once they were inside.

"What?"

"More stairs." Everywhere Megan looked, there were stairs.

"Look over there." Tara pointed to the left. "Elevators."

"Whew. Hey. How come you're not winded at all?"

"I chase four-year-olds around all day. I'm used to this kind of stuff."

"Four-year-olds?" Megan asked. "Like kids in your neighborhood? What do you do when you catch them? I can't image they can run that much faster than you."

"I'm a pre-K teacher. And those kids do move faster than I do. Speaking of which, I don't know what you do for a living." She paused and looked up. "Wow. Look at those tapestries. Can you imagine how much work went into those?"

Megan followed Tara's gaze. She was right. The extraordinarily large tapestries on the wall were beautiful and so intricate. They looked like they would have taken many hours—maybe years—to make.

The first room they went into held a glass case with hand-painted plates and vases. Framed paintings lined the walls. "What do you suppose the artist was trying to say with this one?" Tara asked Megan. She read the card. *Portrait of Cardinal Filippo Archinto.*

The painting was of an old man dressed in a red cloak over a white robe. Half of the painting was a hanging piece of gauze that covered half of the man, obscuring most of his features.

"I think the artist was trying to convey the fact that religion hides behind a curtain."

"Wow," Tara replied. "That's very deep. Is that what you believe?"

"I don't believe in organized religion. I think it was invented as a way to try to control people. You know, keep the masses in line with threats of damnation."

Tara knew that was true in her own life with her parents. She'd never thought about it as a whole. "Did you grow up in a religious family?"

"Nope. Don't get me wrong. My family has a great belief system, but it's much more spiritual than religious. No dogma. No man-made rules."

Tara took a seat on the bench in front of the painting. "What's the difference between religion and spirituality? I always thought they were the same."

"Some people—I guess some religious people—think that following a religion makes them spiritual. But true spiritual people don't need a church and its rules. They…" She paused. "Maybe I should say *I* can give you my beliefs about what it means. I believe in a connection to nature and knowing that we are all one. Every person, animal, plant, everything is connected. Everything we do affects the whole. Does that make sense?"

"I never thought of it that way."

"It's like religion—to me—is a box. And spirituality is everything outside that box." Megan sat down next to Tara.

"Do you believe in God?" Tara asked.

"God, Source, the Universe. Whatever you want to call it, yes, I believe in a creator. But I don't believe in a God that sits on a throne handing out judgments." She pointed around. "You get to go to heaven because you saved a puppy. You have to go to hell because you masturbated."

Tara burst out laughing. "I'm sorry," she said when she got herself under control. "If my parents could hear you talk, they would tell you you were going to hell for even saying that word."

"Masturbation? It's a perfectly good word. It doesn't hurt anyone, and as Woody Allen once said in a movie, it's having sex with someone you love. Or at least you should love yourself." She paused and turned serious. "Do you love yourself, Tara?"

She had to think about that one, and it took her several long moments to answer. She certainly didn't love herself when she was growing up. How could she when her parents constantly told her how bad she was? Did she love herself now? "Sometimes," she said.

"Only sometimes? Why? What are the times you don't love yourself?"

"I don't know. I guess when I think about being cheated on, for one thing. How about you? You were cheated on. Did it make you doubt yourself?"

"No. I'm not the one with the problem. Aliza was. I didn't do anything to deserve what she did to me. Do you think you did something to cause Michael to stray?"

"I've thought about that a lot. I believe I've been a good wife."

"Then your answer is no, but you still feel bad about yourself. Now, how does that make sense?" Megan asked.

Tara shook her head. Megan had a point, but there were so many other reasons she didn't love herself at times. Being told she was no good since she was a child played a big part in that. Reason, no matter how sound, wasn't going to change that in an instant. "It doesn't," Tara replied. She stood. "Shall we continue?"

"Way to change the subject," Megan said with a laugh. She took the hand Tara offered and allowed herself to be pulled up.

They silently walked around the room, Tara thinking more about their brief conversation than the paintings in front of her.

"I'm sorry," Megan said as they moved on to the next room.

"For what?"

"You've been quiet. I'm sorry if I offended you."

Tara did her best to give her a reassuring smile. "You didn't. You've just given me a lot to think about."

"Then I'm sorry I made you think. If there's one thing I hate, it's thinking."

Tara couldn't help but laugh. "I get the feeling you do an awful lot of thinking. I tend to overthink."

"Revolving thoughts? Been there, done that. It got me nowhere. Where does it get you?"

"Back to where I started. How did you get it to stop?" Was there a way to get it to stop?

"It was a process for sure. Every time I realized I was doing it, I stopped and literally put my arms up and surrendered the thoughts to the Universe." She put her arms up to demonstrate. "I mean, I know it sounds weird, but by surrendering it instead of fighting it, it helped."

"It does sound a little weird, but I guess it's worth a try." She continued through the room with Megan close behind. She paused at a large window, moved the curtain, and peered out. The snow had intensified.

"Still snowing?" Megan asked.

"Yeah. It's getting worse." She turned to Megan. "I'm a little worried about driving back in this."

"Do you think we should leave now, before it gets worse?"

Tara shook her head. "We're here now. May as well stay. Hopefully it lets up. Besides," she said, linking her arm in Megan's, "I want to see the rest of this artwork. I'm wondering how many religious paintings there actually are. I think the old masters were a little obsessed with it." She was aware of the close contact between them and was torn between wanting it—wanting more—and needing to pull away because she wanted it.

"I'm going to have to agree with you on that one. It's interesting how much extra detail and items they put into some of the paintings, fruit, dogs, naked people. Some of these paintings are so violent too, which should be the opposite of what religion is supposed to stand for."

"Not according to my parents. They go hand in hand. They insisted God wanted them to physically punish me. Often."

"I'm so sorry."

"Nope. I'm sorry. I shouldn't have brought that up. We are here to have a good time, and I intend to do that." She let go of Megan's arm—reluctantly—and led them into the next room.

"I can't believe how big this place is," Megan said when they'd finished going through the first level. They took the elevator to the second floor. There seemed to be even more people on that level. They weaved their way through the rooms, taking in the art and beautiful objects on display.

"Are you getting hungry?" Tara asked Megan as they finished the third floor.

"Starving," Megan replied. "Do they have a café here?"

"We can do better than that. Have you ever been to the Hard Rock Café?"

"I have not. I'm assuming you have."

Tara pressed the button for the elevator. "I have not. Nor have I ever been to Philadelphia before. I wanted to have a new adventure today."

Megan's face lit up. Dimples. "I am honored that you wanted to share it with me."

"New friend. New adventure. What could be better?"

The elevator door opened and a throng of people streamed out—and a new throng, including Tara and Megan, piled in.

The snow was still coming down as they walked to the car, and the traffic was thick and slow-going on the way to the restaurant. It wasn't nearly as crowded as Tara thought it would be when they finally arrived, and they only had a fifteen-minute wait to be seated.

The food was as good as Tara expected. What she hadn't expected was how bad the weather was when they walked back to the car. Tara pulled up the weather app on her phone. "It looks like it's still snowing all the way back home. I don't think I want to drive in this."

"Do you want me to drive?" Megan asked.

"No. Do you have anything you need to get back for tonight? What would you think if we got a couple of rooms for the night?"

"I made sure Dozer had plenty of food and water. He'll be okay. To be honest with you, I was just being nice. I wouldn't want to drive in this weather either."

"It's settled, then." Tara did a google search for nearby hotels. The drive there felt like they were crawling. There was less traffic on the road, which she was thankful for.

"I'm sorry," the clerk behind the hotel desk said. "We only have one room available, and that's only because someone canceled twenty minutes ago. I'm sure it will be snatched up soon if you don't take it. The hotels are pretty much booked up. We have two major conventions in town, not to mention people that are here for the Eagles game."

Tara turned to Megan. "What do you think?"

"I think we can deal with having one room. I wouldn't risk losing it by trying other hotels."

Tara turned back to the clerk. "We'll take it." She filled out the paperwork and handed him her credit card. She received two room key cards in return.

"Would you like help with your luggage?" the clerk asked.

"We don't have any. We weren't planning on getting stranded in Philadelphia because of the weather."

"In that case we can send up personal supplies, toothbrushes and such if you would like."

"Oh, yes. That would be truly appreciated," Tara responded.

"No problem. The elevators are to your right."

Tara thanked him and followed Megan to the elevator, a man stepped in just before the doors closed. Tara was sure she had seen him in the museum as well. She figured there must be a lot of guests here who also visited the museum. Their room was almost directly across from the elevator on the third floor. The clerk hadn't mentioned if the room had one or two beds. She silently prayed there were two.

She put her key card up to the sensor and opened the door. "One bed," she said. She hadn't meant to say it out loud, but it just slipped out.

"I can sleep in the bathtub." Megan said.

Tara couldn't tell if she was joking or not. "You will not."

"Oh good. I wasn't looking forward to that, anyway."

Megan closed the door behind them. "Is it okay if I turn the heat up? It's freezing in here."

"Of course. Whatever you need." Tara took in the room. There was a big window with heavy drapes and a set of sheer curtains behind it, a desk with a lamp and chair, and an upholstered chair in the corner. The TV set was large and was mounted on the wall above a long dresser, and there was a small nightstand next to the bed. At least it was a queen-size bed and not a full. If she slept close to the edge there would be very little chance of them touching each other. The thought of that sent a surge through her that she was sure made her wet. She made a beeline to the bathroom, shut the door, and leaned against it. This will be fine, she told herself. She'd slept in the same bed as her sister and even Cori before. Of course, she wasn't attracted to them. She was, she admitted to herself, attracted to Megan.

She splashed cold water on her face hoping that would help. It only sent a cold chill down her spine. She laughed out loud when she looked over and realized there was a shower but no bathtub. It was an open design with cream colored porcelain tiles and brass fixtures. She opened the bathroom door to find Megan bending over, looking into the small refrigerator that Tara had failed to notice before. "You couldn't sleep in the bathtub, even if you wanted to."

"Why? Is it disgusting?" Megan asked.

"No. It's nonexistent."

"What? Who ever heard of a hotel room without a bathtub?"

"There is a shower. A huge, opened shower," Tara said.

"Opened? As in no doors or shower curtain?"

"Come and look." Tara stepped out of the way so Megan could go past her without making physical contact. She smelled a light scent of vanilla and something else—maybe honeysuckle—as Megan went past her. She wondered why she hadn't noticed it before.

"Wow," Megan said. "I love it."

"It is nice, isn't it?"

Megan turned to her. "There are plenty of small bottles of alcohol in the fridge if you want a drink."

Tara wasn't sure if that would help or make things worse. "Are you going to have one?"

"If you are, I will."

"Oh no. We aren't playing that game. If you want a drink, have a drink. And…" She let the word linger for a couple of seconds. "I will have a drink."

Megan laughed. "Okay then."

"What are our choices?"

Megan crouched down and opened the mini fridge. She moved a few bottles and cans around. "I'm no bartender, but I think we can make gin and tonic, rum and Coke, a screwdriver, or a Bloody Mary if we use V8 juice."

Tara sat in the office chair by the desk. "What sounds good to you?"

"Oh no. We aren't playing that game," Megan said, and Tara could tell she was smiling even though she couldn't see her face.

"How gross do you think it would be to make a Bloody Mary with V8?"

"Only semi-gross," Megan answered.

"Then I'll have that. I can deal with semi-gross. What are you going to have?"

Megan put the can of V8 and the small bottle of vodka on the desk. "I'm going to have a screwdriver."

Three drinks and four bags of potato chips later, they were propped up in bed watching *The Wedding Singer* on the big screen TV. "You know," Megan said, "this might not have been the best choice for a movie."

"Why?"

"Because your marriage went to shit." Megan paused. "Because your marriage went to shit because of me. I'm sorry."

"But I love Drew Barrymore. And you are not the reason my marriage went to shit. Michael is. And I am."

"You aren't," Megan insisted. "You aren't the one that cheated."

"But I never really had both feet in it," Tara replied.

"Where were your feet?" Megan giggled. She was so cute when she was tipsy. Or was she drunk?

Tara was sure she herself was a little more than tipsy. "My feet were…My feet were somewhere else. I mean, one foot was in the marriage. The other foot wanted to wander."

"Wander where?" Megan asked. "Did you cheat?"

"Never."

"Then where did your foot wander?"

"My mind wondered. My foot actually stayed home, in my marriage."

"Where did your mind wander?"

That was something Tara never planned on telling her. "To women." Oh, there it was. She'd said it. Damn alcohol.

"What does that mean?"

Tara wasn't sure how much to say. The alcohol seemed to have other ideas. "It means I've always liked women. Not so much men. I don't mean I hate men. There are some men that I like very much. I just like women. I don't like like men. Do you know what I mean? I feel like I'm not making any sense."

Megan sat up straight. "Wait. You like like women, but you married Michael? Why?"

Tara felt like she'd already said too much. "Never mind."

"Oh no. We aren't never minding this. You just told me you're a lesbian."

Tara paused the movie. "I never used that word."

"So, what are you if you like like woman? A woman liker?"

Tara laughed. "Yes. I'm a woman liker. I don't have my hair cropped or wear combat boots. So I don't fit the lesbian mold."

"Are you being serious right now? That is not a lesbian mold. A lesbian can be anything, wear anything, have their hair any way they want."

"I'm just kidding. I shouldn't have said anything. It's a secret that I've only told Cori. She's my best friend." Was she slurring her words? She didn't think so. She sounded totally normal. "So, you can't tell anyone."

"Why did you marry Michael?"

"You like women. Or at least you had a girlfriend, and you dated Michael. Why was that? Maybe Michael just attracts women who like like women?" She laughed again at the thought of it. Yeah, drinking alcohol was a mistake. She couldn't seem to keep her secrets to herself.

"I like women and men, but to be honest I like women more. I wasn't really serious about Michael. You are the one that married him."

"Are you mad at me now?" Tara couldn't tell by the tone of Megan's voice.

"No. I like you. I'm not mad."

Tara wondered if she like liked her, but didn't dare ask. It would be a bad situation if they like liked each other and were alone in a hotel room with one bed and alcohol flowing through them.

"I'm getting tired," Tara said, trying to get out of this conversation before something happened.

"It's only eight o'clock," Megan said.

"Maybe I get tired at eight o'clock."

"Why did you marry Michael?" Megan asked again. She obviously wasn't going to let it go.

"Because my parents wanted me to." It was the truth.

"What? Wait. Your parents wanted you to and you did?"

"I also wanted to get away from them, so it seemed like a win-win situation."

"Did you love him?"

Tara slipped off the bed. "I have to go to the bathroom," she said. That was also the truth.

She felt a little unsteady on her feet. Maybe more than a little. In the bathroom, she did her business and took her time washing her hands. She shouldn't have told Megan that she liked women. She certainly couldn't tell that she liked her and was starting to really like her. That would just be wrong, she wasn't exactly sure why, but she also knew she wasn't thinking clearly after drinking. That was just plain stupid. She ripped the plastic wrap off the glass on the sink, filled it with water, and drank it. The last thing she needed was a headache in the morning. She refilled it and brought it to Megan. She handed it to her without comment.

"Thanks." Megan drank the water and set the glass on the desk next to her.

Tara put her finger to her lips. She climbed back onto the bed. "Shh. I have to call Michael and tell him I'm not coming home tonight."

"Where did you tell him you were today?"

"I told him I was going to Philadelphia with a friend. He didn't ask who."

"What would you have told him if he did ask?"

"I don't know. I was just relieved he didn't," Tara replied. "The hell with it. I'm just going to text him. You can talk." She grabbed her phone off the nightstand next to her. *The weather got bad here, so I got a hotel room for the night. I'll see you tomorrow.*

She returned the phone to the nightstand and turned toward

Megan. Megan smiled at her. Dimples. She turned away again. She couldn't look at her. Not across a bed anyway. "I thought I could grow to love him."

"What?"

"You asked me before I went to the bathroom if I loved Michael. I didn't when I married him. I thought I could grow to love him. I did care about him. I guess that makes me a horrible person."

Megan put a hand on Tara's shoulder. Tara did her best to ignore it. "You are not a horrible person. From the sound of it, your parents were the horrible ones. No one could blame you for needing to get away from them. And you tried to make Michael happy, didn't you?"

Tara turned to look at her and saw the sincerity in her eyes. It brought tears to her own eyes. "I did. I really did." She was afraid she might start crying, and if she did, Megan might try to comfort her. She'd watched enough movies to know what that could lead to. "I have to go to the bathroom again." She needed to put some space between them.

Megan wondered what she had done wrong and why Tara kept running off to the bathroom. She probably shouldn't have touched her. Even if it was just her shoulder. Megan was certainly enjoying their time together, and Tara seemed to be too. Tara was probably embarrassed at the confession she made. Megan had some confessions of her own, but there was no way, alcohol flowing through her or not, she would ever confess that she was developing feelings for her.

Tara's phone on the nightstand pinged. Megan had the urge to look at it but didn't. "I think you have a text," she said when Tara returned after what seemed like forever but was probably only a few minutes. Her eyes looked like she had been crying. "You okay?"

"Yep." She picked up her phone and looked at it. "Oh, that's nice. He doesn't respond for almost a half hour and just says 'okay.'"

"A man of few words."

Tara sat on the edge of the bed and looked at Megan. "He has been—a man of few words—with me lately. Was he like that with you?"

Megan was embarrassed to say no. "He talked a lot, but I now know most of it was lies. He told me stuff about his sick mom and his job as a pilot that didn't exist."

Tara slid all the way on the bed but stayed close to the edge. It didn't escape Megan's notice. "What did he say about his mother?" Tara asked.

Megan had to think about it for several moments. She had been trying to forget everything about Mike since finding out about Tara, especially when she started having feelings for her. Knowing they were married, even if she planned on divorcing him, hurt. "He said she owned a gift shop that she inherited from her father. She grew up in North Carolina and moved to New York after meeting his father who was in the service, and they got married." She stopped talking when she noticed the sad look on Tara's face. "I'm sorry. What is it?"

"All of that is true." She suddenly laughed. "He told you the truth about his mom. Lied about his job. Lied about me."

Megan was confused. "Why is that funny?"

"It's not. That's what makes it funny. I think I've had too much to drink." She looked at her phone that was still in her hand and started typing.

"What are you doing?" Megan asked.

"I want to know if vodka affects you differently than wine. I usually drink wine. I think the vodka makes me feel different." She took a minute or two to scroll through the results and then put her phone on the bed between them.

"So? What does it say?"

"One site said no, and another one said it can. So, the answer is who the hell knows. Who the hell knows about anything?"

Megan didn't like the shift the conversation and the direction the general mood seemed to be taking. She wanted to enjoy their time together and have Tara feel the same. Tara's mood seemed to be all over the place.

"Is there any vodka left? I'm thinking of having another drink. Maybe it will even me out."

Megan shook her head. "No."

"How about anything else? I can do a science experiment. See if gin makes me feel different than wine or vodka."

Alcohol was the last thing Tara seemed to need, Megan thought. "Doesn't mixing different kinds of alcohol make you sick?" She wasn't sure if that was true or not, but she didn't want Tara to get more tipsy than she already was.

"What about things like a Long Island iced tea? There are like ten different types of booze in that. Never mind. I'm going to lie down." She scootched down and laid her head on the pillow.

The knock on the door pulled Megan's attention from Tara. She looked through the peephole. The man outside the door seemed to be holding towels and toothbrushes. She opened the door, accepted the toiletries, and thanked him. Tara was asleep when she turned around. That was probably for the best. They'd had a good—great—day up until the last half hour or so. She wasn't sure what to make of Tara's changing moods. She chalked it up to a combination of alcohol and her feelings about Michael.

Megan deposited the toiletries in the bathroom. She gently removed Tara's shoes and took the covers from her side of the bed to cover Tara up. She climbed back on the bed and looked over at her and was flooded with feelings of her own. Tara had admitted to—how did she phrase it—like liking women. Did that change anything between them? Megan wasn't sure. Tara gave no indication that she felt that way about Megan. And why would she? Megan was the one that broke up her marriage. A marriage that seemed to be full of lies. Many lies from Michael and one big one from Tara. Megan was still mulling the newfound facts over in her mind when she drifted off to sleep. She woke up before dawn from a dream of making love to Tara. Her body was on fire. How easy it would be to reach over and touch her. She knew it was something she could never do. She slipped out of bed and sat in the chair to put distance between them and quell the want. It didn't help.

Chapter Nine

The pounding in Tara's head startled her awake. It took her several long moments to realize where she was. She rolled over expecting to see Megan sleeping next to her. She was surprised to see her slumped back in the chair sleeping.

She got up slowly and was grateful to see a tube of toothpaste and two toothbrushes on the bathroom sink. Brushing her teeth did little to remove the nasty taste in her mouth.

The thought of food turned her stomach, but she thought some caffeine might help quell the pounding in her head. She weighed the option of making coffee in the small pot that was in the room or going downstairs in search of some. She chose the latter, opting for the ability to add cream and sugar as opposed to the powdered creamer in the tiny packets near the coffee maker. She silently slipped out of the room and was surprised to run into the same man that had ridden up in the elevator the day before.

"Hello," she said to him. He nodded in return as they rode down to the lobby.

She followed the sign that pointed in the direction of the café and found what she was looking for. After pouring coffee into two Styrofoam cups and adding cream and sugar, she put plastic lids on top. She spotted donuts on her way out and grabbed one for Megan.

Megan was awake and in the bathroom when she returned to the room. She sat at the desk and sipped her coffee. It warmed her stomach and kick-started her brain. *Oh, shit. I told Megan I'm gay.* She mentally kicked herself for that. What else had she admitted to? Did she tell Megan she had feelings for her? She didn't think so but wasn't sure. She knew drinking was a bad idea but had done it anyway. How stupid could she be? Very, was the answer.

"Hey there," Megan said as she exited the bathroom. "How are you doing?"

"Feeling very embarrassed." *And stupid.*

"Why?"

Tara held up one of the Styrofoam cups. "I brought you coffee and a donut."

"You're great at evading questions, you know that?"

"Am I?"

"That proves my point. Let's go back to the original question. Why are you feeling embarrassed? Because of how much you drank? 'Cause I matched you drink for drink."

"For what I said." Tara hoped that she wouldn't have to clarify her answer.

Megan crossed the room and took the cup of coffee Tara offered her. She waved off the offer of a donut. "Don't worry about it. I won't tell anyone."

Tara was worried more about the fact that she had told Megan than worried about her telling. She didn't think Megan would do that.

"Is there something else?" Megan asked.

Tara shook her head. Ow. That hurt. She just wanted the whole subject dropped.

"Did you check the weather this morning?"

"No. Did you?" Tara responded.

Megan shook her head and opened the drapes. "It's sunny and clear," she declared.

Tara shielded her eyes against the bright light. "How come you aren't hung over?" she asked.

"I am. Sort of sick to my stomach. But not too bad. You don't feel good?"

"My head is pounding."

"Did you take anything for it?"

Tara held up her coffee. "Just this."

Megan set her cup on the desk. "I'll go find you something. Any preference? Aspirin, Tylenol, Advil?"

Tara felt guilty making Megan go get her medicine. But her need for relief outweighed it. "Advil if you can find it. Anything else if you can't. I really appreciate it."

"Of course," Megan said and headed out the door.

Tara looked up the weather forecast on her phone. It looked like it would be a nice day. If she could just get rid of this headache, she could enjoy it. The caffeine was beginning to help by the time Megan reappeared with her medicine.

"Victory," she said, holding up a small package of Advil. She pulled another one from her pocket and placed both on the desk in front of Tara. "And one for later if you need it."

"Thank you so much." She downed the two tablets with her coffee. "If I can get rid of this headache, would you like to continue our tour of Philadelphia?"

"I would," Megan replied. "I would love to see the Liberty Bell. Do you want to lie back down for a while? Maybe take a nap?"

That didn't sound like a bad idea and might be just what she needed. "I don't want to ruin your day by sleeping." She silently hoped Megan would object. That would ease some of her guilt at holding up their day.

"Nonsense. I don't want to sightsee if you're not feeling well. You take a nap. I'm going to go for a walk and just take in the fresh air."

"I'm not going to argue with that. Make sure you know your way back. I would hate for you to get lost."

Megan smiled. Damn those dimples. Why did they have to pop out so often? She held up her phone. "I have an app that can mark my starting point aka this hotel, and it will get me back here no matter how far I wander. What do you think? Maybe an hour? Is that enough time?"

"Perfect. Please don't let me sleep longer than that."

"You got it." Megan grabbed her coat from the small open closet by the door. "Drink some water before you lie down," she said and went out the door.

There was a man at the end of the hallway that she was sure she'd seen before. She just couldn't place where. She shook it off as her being silly. Of course she didn't know anyone in Philadelphia. She took the elevator down to the main lobby and walked outside. She squinted against the bright sun bouncing off the fresh snow. It took her eyes several long moments to adjust, and she considered going to the hotel gift shop to see if they had sunglasses. She decided against the idea and continued down Filbert Street, where she took a left and kept going around the block. There was a café, a bakery, and a jewelry store. When she came to a small gift shop, she went in.

The saleswoman greeted her with a smile. She wanted to get something for Tara to show her appreciation for the trip but had no idea what. She felt like they had become fast friends but still felt like she didn't know her that well. Yet. She hoped that would change.

"Can I help you find anything?" the clerk asked. She pushed several strands of gray hair behind her ear.

"I'm not sure. I want to get a gift for a friend, but I'm at a loss."

"What type of things does your friend like?"

Megan shook her head. "That's the thing. She's a very new friend and I don't know." *Women. She likes women.* That revelation sprang to her mind and she smiled to herself. If they hadn't been drinking, she was sure Tara wouldn't have told her that. But she couldn't get her anything along those lines. Any and all rainbow items were out of the question.

"We have some lovely handmade soap over here." She led Megan to a small table in the center of the store. It smelled heavenly. "And a nice collection of Mackenzie-Childs items toward the back if that is more her style." Megan didn't think so.

"How much is the soap?" she asked.

"Twelve dollars a bar."

That seemed like a lot of money for a bar of soap, but if anyone was worth it, Tara was. "I'll take this one," she said, picking up a bar of Rosemary Sage. "And this Creamsicle. Would you happen to do gift wrapping?"

"I'm sorry. We don't. But our bags are cute enough to use as gift bags." She led the way over to the cash register and rang up the sale. She gently wrapped each bar of soap in colored tissue paper, placed it into a bag covered with a bright sunflower design, and handed it to Megan. Megan thanked her and was on her way once again.

She stopped at a pet store to look at the puppies and kittens and was happy to see they were from shelters and not from puppy mills or breeders.

She returned to the hotel to find the same man that was at the end of the hall earlier, but he was now sitting in the lobby. He still struck her as looking familiar, but it wasn't worth dwelling on.

Tara was taking a shower when Megan got back up to the room. At least it sounded like she was. The donut sitting on a napkin on the desk looked too good to resist, and she took a large bite. She heard the water shut off in the bathroom, and a couple minutes later, Tara emerged with wet messy hair and a bathrobe wrapped loosely around her, a good amount of cleavage in view. The sight made Megan's mouth go dry. How could someone in only a robe look so damn good? Maybe it was *because* she was only in a robe that she looked so appealing. Megan tried to look away but found she couldn't. She scanned the entire length of Tara and ended on her eyes. Tara was looking at Megan just as intently as she seemed to be looking at her. Megan swallowed hard.

"How was your walk?" Tara asked. Breaking the spell.

"Um. Yeah. It was good. Still cold out but the sun is nice, and it isn't snowing and the sidewalks are shoveled and there are some nice shops around here and in fact I got you something." That was way too many words to put into one sentence. What the hell was wrong with her? It wasn't like it was the first time she'd been alone with a beautiful woman. It was the first time she'd been in a hotel room with Tara who was naked under that robe. *Stop. It.* She brought her attention to the bag she'd placed on the bed when she got back.

"You did, huh? You didn't have to do that."

"I probably would have resented it if I felt I *had* to do that."

"We wouldn't want that, now, would we? What did you get me?" Tara put her hand up. "No. Wait. Let me get dressed first." She returned to the bathroom and shut the door.

Megan hit the heal of her hand against her forehead. "Stop. Stop. Stop."

Tara got dressed in record time. She hadn't heard Megan return and hadn't intended to step out of the bathroom in just a robe. The intense way Megan had looked at her made her feel—what? Wanted? Was that it? It had been so long since someone wanted her, she'd forgotten how it felt. Was it possible that Megan wanted her as much as she wanted Megan? It didn't matter. Nothing could happen between them. Not now anyway. She was still legally and morally married. Did the morality part count anymore, seeing Michael had cheated? She thought it did. At least for her.

"What did you get me?" Tara said as she emerged from the bathroom.

"You're like a little kid on Christmas." Megan smiled.

"Is that a bad thing?" Tara wanted to concentrate on anything but her feelings.

"No. It's cute." Megan pointed to the small bag on the bed. "All yours. I wanted to show you how grateful I am for this trip."

Tara peered into the bag and was greeted with the most heavenly scent. "I love it," she said after she pulled the soaps from the bag. "Thank you. That was very thoughtful." She wanted to hug Megan for the gift but thought better of it. Physical contact when her feelings were running so high was a bad idea. "Shall we get going?" The sooner they got out of this intimate room, the better. "Did you want to stop at the café downstairs for breakfast?" Tara asked.

"I ate the donut you brought me. But we should stop so you can eat."

"My stomach is still saying no to that. Are you sure you had enough?"

"Absolutely." Megan rose and grabbed both of their coats from the closet. She held Tara's for her and Tara stepped into it.

The rest of their day and the drive home was fairly quiet. Tara wondered if Megan was feeling the way she was and knew they needed a little more space between them. Their friendship had developed so quickly, and Tara suspected that if they weren't careful, more would develop just as fast. She couldn't let that happen. She could only hope Megan realized that too.

Chapter Ten

Y ou did what?" Cori asked Tara.

"You heard me. What part didn't you understand?" Tara sipped her wine. An evening with Cori while her husband was away on a business trip was just what she needed.

"I guess I don't understand why you would invite her to go to Philly with you."

"I feel like I owe her for helping me. She's never really traveled, and I thought it would be nice for her."

"That's the story you're telling yourself?" Cori leaned forward in her chair.

"It's the truth," Tara insisted. Not the whole truth, but enough of it.

"Start over. You invited her. She accepted. And then what?"

"We went to the museum, talked about the art, ate dinner, and then went to the hotel. We didn't have a choice. It was only supposed to be a day trip, but you know how the weather was. The snow was bad, and driving home would have been too dangerous." She always told Cori everything, but sharing the details of her feelings and her confession to Megan proved to be too difficult. She wasn't sure why.

"Did you get separate rooms?"

There was no way to avoid answering the question, not with the way Cori was staring at her. "There was only one room available."

"You're telling me there was only one hotel room in the whole city of Philadelphia?" The sarcasm in her voice was evident.

Tara explained what the hotel clerk had told her. "We were afraid that if we didn't take it and checked with other places, we wouldn't have a room at all. It wasn't like we planned it."

"And?" Cori asked.

"And what?"

"And what happened? You spent the night with this woman. This woman I know you like—more than you're willing to admit to me. Tara, why is this like pulling teeth? Tell me what happened."

"Nothing happened." But it certainly could have. Tara was sure of that. She shook her head. There was no sense withholding information from Cori when she could just about read Tara's mind. "There was only one bed in the room, and we helped ourselves to the drinks in the mini fridge. Three drinks later and I told her about me."

"That you're gay?" Cori's eyes opened wide. "You told her that? It took you how many years to tell me, and you've known this woman for how long?"

"I wish you would stop calling her *this woman*. Her name is Megan." Tara took a long swig of her wine. She needed the lubrication if she was going to be honest with Cori. Apparently, alcohol helped with that.

"You barely know this wo—Megan and you take her on a trip, spend the night with her, and tell her you're gay. I will never fail to be amazed by you."

"Amazed or disgusted?" Tara couldn't tell.

"Oh, honey, I could never be disgusted by you. I'm just shocked by all this. You didn't even tell me you were going to Philadelphia. You used to tell me everything."

"I'm telling you now."

"Did anything else happen?"

"Are you asking me if I slept with her?" Tara knew damn well that was what she was asking. "We did sleep in the same bed. But nothing else happened."

"Did you want it to?" Cori asked.

Did she want it to? That was the question. She knew how

much she liked Megan and how attracted to her she was. Would she have made love to her under different circumstances? If she wasn't married? Probably. Yes. "I don't know."

"What does that mean? You either wanted to or you didn't."

Tara leaned back and looked up at the ceiling as if the answer was written there. "It's all so complicated."

Cori agreed. "It certainly is unusual. I'll give you that."

"That, my friend, is an understatement."

"Did Michael know you went to Philadelphia with her?"

"Of course not. He doesn't know I called her or that I even know her. I need to keep that secret until I'm actually going for the divorce." She grabbed a cracker from the plate in front of her. She hadn't touched the snacks Cori had placed on the small table between them since they sat down. Drinking wine on an empty stomach might not be the best idea.

"And how is that going?"

"I have a meeting with my lawyer tomorrow. I'll find out more then. I don't want to be living with Michael when he's served the papers." She wasn't sure what his reaction would be, and she certainly didn't want to find out if they were in the same house.

"Do you want to stay here?" Cori asked.

Tara found herself tearing up at the offer. She was so grateful to have such a good friend. "I appreciate that. I might take you up on it. I want to talk to my sister first. I don't want to move out too soon. I need to find out when he can be served. I'm hoping my lawyer can tell me that tomorrow."

"Of course. It's a standing offer. You are always welcome here."

"Thank you for that."

The doorbell rang and Cori got up to answer it. She returned with a large pizza box. "Dinner has arrived." She set it on the coffee table, went to the kitchen, and returned with plates and napkins. She poured more wine into both of their glasses before she returned to her seat. "Help yourself." She waited until Tara retrieved a piece of pizza before putting one on her own plate.

"Feel like answering my question now?" Cori said between bites.

"I thought I answered all your questions."

"Did you want to more than *sleep* with her? With Megan?"

"I answered that." Tara grabbed a napkin and wiped a bit of sauce from her lips.

"You said you don't know and it's complicated. But that's not really an answer."

"It is if I really don't know." She paused. "Okay. I really like her. And yes, I'm attracted to her. But it needs to stop there."

"Do you think she has feelings for you?"

Tara thought back to the way Megan looked at her when she came out of the bathroom in just a bathrobe. She thought so then, but looks can be deceiving, as the saying goes. Maybe Megan was just surprised to see her that way. But just thinking about the way they stared at each other for what seemed like an eternity wrapped up in a few seconds made her stomach flip. "I think she might."

"Does that complicate things?" Cori took a bite of pizza and washed it down with her wine.

"Not for me. Nothing can happen between us. So it's a moot point."

"Nothing is moot when two people have feelings for each other."

Tara laughed. "What kind of messed-up philosophy is that?"

"I don't know. It sounded good in my head," Cori said. "What do you plan on doing?"

"Nothing," Tara responded. "Absolutely nothing."

❖

"And just sign and date this last one here." Jackson pointed to the line on the bottom of the paperwork.

Tara signed her name, put the date, and handed the stack of stapled papers back to her lawyer. "Now what?" she asked.

"Now I file with the court and serve your husband."

"How long will that take?"

"I'll file the papers tomorrow and Michael will be served sometime next week. The time frame depends on the process server's schedule. He's pretty good about it. Michael then has twenty days to respond. If he doesn't respond, we proceed, and your divorce is granted by the courts." He explained the time frame they could expect if that was the case. "If he objects to either the divorce or the terms of the prenup, we then try to reach a settlement. If that doesn't work, we go to court and a judge decides."

Tara prayed that that wasn't the case. He couldn't object if she had solid proof that he had cheated. And she had Megan in her corner for that.

"Can you let me know when you know the time frame? I'm going to stay with my sister while all this is happening and want to go there at least a day or two before Michael knows what's going on."

"Will do. Can I get your sister's address? Your legal address will stay the same for now. Is that right?"

Tara nodded. "Yes. Staying with my sister is just temporary." She rattled off the address while Jackson typed it into his computer. "Also," he said. "I'd like to get…" He flipped up a page on his legal pad. "Megan back in here to go over her statement again and have her sign an affidavit. You can give her a call, or I can if that works better for you."

"No. I can do it."

"Great. I'd like you both to come in at the same time, if possible, so you know exactly what's going on and what to expect from her."

They wrapped up the meeting and Tara headed out to her car. She just wanted this to be over. She'd already talked to her sister and Anna said she could stay as long as she needed. She hadn't told Michael yet. She wasn't sure how much of her stuff to take. Damn, she thought. *I should have asked Jackson if I left stuff at the house for now, could I get it later or would it be considered abandoned.* She'd have to call him later and ask. There was so much more to this than she had anticipated.

She called Megan once she was back in her car.

"Hi, Tara."

"Hi. I just left the lawyer's office and signed all the papers."

"How are you doing?" Megan asked. "I can only imagine how hard this is for you. What can I do to make it easier?"

Stop being so nice, Tara thought. *So I can stop having feelings for you.* "Jackson wanted us both to come back in so he can go over some stuff with you. Is that a possibility?" Tara started the car and got a blast of cold air from the heater. She quickly turned it off.

"Of course," Megan said. "When?"

"We didn't set anything up yet. I wasn't sure when you're free. You know, with all the talking we've done, I've never even asked you what your schedule is. I'm sorry. That was so wrong on my part." It had just never come up in their conversations.

"Stop. It's fine. I can text you my work schedule…or…you can come over for dinner and we can go over it then."

As much as Tara wanted to spend more time with Megan, she wasn't sure it was a good idea—especially if they were alone.

"Ooor not," Megan said when Tara didn't answer,

"What time?" Shit. When had she lost control of her mouth? Or was it her brain?

"Anytime? We can eat around six if that's not too early for you."

"It's not. Let's see, it's…" She looked at the time on her car. "Four twenty now. So how about I run some errands and come over about five?"

"Perfect. Anything in particular you would like to eat?"

Now there's a loaded question, Tara thought and immediately reprimanded herself. She was glad Megan couldn't read her mind.

"Tara? Still there?"

"I'm sure whatever you make will be fine. I'll be there by five."

"Great. I'm home now, so if you get done earlier, come on over. See you soon. Bye."

"Bye," Tara squeaked out. *Why can I not resist being with this woman? I'm supposed to hate the woman that slept with my husband. Not crave her myself. How sick am I?*

She didn't really have errands to run, she just wanted to buy herself more time. Her head was swimming from the meeting she'd just left. As much as she wanted—no, needed—to divorce Michael, it was all so hard. She was about to be displaced from the only home she'd known other than the hellhole she grew up in. It was her choice, she knew. But she couldn't keep living a lie. The lie that her marriage to Michael was happy and the lie that she should be with a man at all. She felt like her life was dissolving before her and at the same time some of the pieces seemed to be falling into place. She just hoped they fell in an order she could live with.

❖

She drove around aimlessly for a while, overthinking everything. It was four fifty-nine when she pulled into the parking lot of Megan's apartment building. She did her best to ignore the knot in her stomach as she knocked on Megan's door. Was it excitement or dread? *Who knows.* It disappeared as soon as Megan opened the door. Not sure if it was wise or not, she hugged her. And more than that. Megan hugged her back. It felt good to be wrapped in her arms. Calming. Right.

"Are you okay?" Megan said so close to Tara's ear that a shiver ran down her back and her stomach did a flip.

Tara pulled back. "This divorce stuff is taking a lot out of me. I don't think I was truly prepared for the emotional toll."

"Come in and sit down. I'll pour you a glass of wine. Wine helps everything." She hung up Tara's coat, led the way to the kitchen table, and pulled out a chair.

Tara sat and watched as Megan retrieved a corkscrew from a drawer and expertly opened a bottle of wine. She poured a glass and placed it in front of her.

"Chardonnay. Not as fancy as the one we had at the restaurant, but I think Kendall-Jackson is a decent brand," Megan said with a smile. She set the bottle in front of Tara. "Just in case one glass isn't enough." She sat across from her. "Are you still certain you want to go through with the divorce?"

"Oh my God, yes," Tara responded. "That's not the issue. It's all the little things." She told Megan her plans to live with her sister for a while. "I want to be out of the house before he's served the divorce papers. I don't know if I should talk to him about leaving or just pack my things and clear out while he's at work. I'll have to eventually find a place to live." Dozer jumped up on her lap, momentarily startling her. "Well, hello there," she said to him. She looked up at Megan. "Maybe I'll get a cat when I get my own place. Michael never wanted animals in the house."

"I'm sorry. Dozer can be so rude. He didn't even ask if he could join us. You can push him off if he's being a pain."

"Not at all. Some furry loving is probably just what I need right now." She smiled and wondered if it was the first time she'd done that since she left work earlier.

"Furry loving? Isn't that some type of fetish?"

Tara laughed. It felt good after the day she'd had. "I don't mean that kind of furry loving."

"I can help you move your stuff."

"I appreciate that, but under the circumstances I don't think you should be anywhere near the house."

"Yeah. I didn't think of that. What else do you have to do?"

"Papers are signed. I don't know if I'll have to go to court or if we can settle this civilly. That kind of freaks me out."

"I'm assuming I would be going to court with you, if that helps any."

"Actually, it does. I feel so alone in this process." She sipped her wine. It was good. "I mean I have you, my sister, and my friend Cori. And I'm very appreciative. But I'm the one getting divorced. I'm the one starting over." She paused and shook her head. "I sound like I'm whining, and I'm sorry."

"Stop," Megan said. "You're going through a lot. Of course some of it is going to freak you out. And yes, you have me, and I'm glad you have your sister and your friend. Tell me what else is going on with you."

"Isn't that enough?"

Megan smiled. Dimples. "It is a lot, but I'm sure there's more. I have two good ears that are just hanging out on the sides of my head. They are great for listening."

"Is that what those two things are? I was wondering."

"I find them very useful. What else?" Megan asked again.

There were so many things that Tara had to take a few moments to sort it out in her mind. "I'm kind of worried about Michael's reaction. I don't think he'll object to the divorce, but he isn't likely to want to part with his money. If it wasn't for my parents pushing for the prenup, he never would have agreed to it. He is the one who insisted that I got nothing if I cheated or left him for no reason."

"Why would he think you would leave him for no reason?"

Tara took a deep breath and blew it out. "I think that was his way of trying to protect his inheritance."

"Are you even allowed to get a divorce without a reason?" Megan asked.

"I have no idea. But why would you? Of course you're going to have a reason. The point is, he will probably fight the prenup."

"You have undisputable proof he cheated. I know you don't want to go to court, but hopefully it won't come to that when he sees that."

"Can we talk about something else? I really need to get my head out of this."

"Of course." Megan rose. "Is it okay if I get dinner started while we chat?"

"What can I help with?" Tara asked.

"Nothing. Sit and relax. I've got this covered." She pulled several things from the refrigerator and set them on the counter.

"What do you do for a living?" Tara asked. She was embarrassed that she hadn't asked her before.

"I'm a podcaster."

"You are?" Tara had never considered that a career.

"You sound surprised." Megan moved one of the racks in the oven to another position and turned the oven on.

"What's the name of it? I'll have to start listening."

"*And Now This.*"

"Now what?" Tara was confused.

"No. That's the name of the show, *And Now This.*"

"Oh. What's it about?"

Megan explained some of the conversations she and Victoria had had on the show. "So, between the three of us, me, Victoria and Lynn—our producer, we come up with topics. Sometimes our listeners email in ideas."

"Do you enjoy it?" Tara asked.

Megan placed two pieces of what Tara assumed were chicken breast between two pieces of plastic wrap. She searched for something in one of the drawers. She paused to answer the question. "I get paid to have a conversation with a friend. I love it." She pulled a meat tenderizer hammer from the drawer. Their chat paused while she pounded on the meat.

Tara absentmindedly ran her hand over Dozer's dark fur. "Sounds like the ideal job," she said once Megan stopped abusing the meat. Tara's phone rang in her pocket, startling her. Dozer leaped off her lap onto the table.

Megan scooped him up and set him on the floor. "You know that's not allowed," she told him.

Tara retrieved her phone and looked at the caller ID. "It's Michael. He almost never calls me anymore."

"Go ahead and get it," Megan replied. "I can go in the other room."

"No. He can just leave a message. I don't even want to think about him right now." The flip her stomach did at the thought of him wasn't very pleasant. Her phone pinged with a text as she was putting it back in her pocket. "It's from him," she announced. "He wants to know where I am because he was expecting me to be home to make him dinner." She let out a sarcastic laugh. He wasn't home for dinner most nights anymore, and the one night she wasn't there he wanted her there to cook for him.

"Are you going to answer him?"

Tara thought about it for a few moments. "I probably should, but I'm not sure what to say."

"Can you just say you're having dinner with a friend? That way you're not lying."

"I never used to lie—to him or anyone else. I don't have a problem lying to him anymore. I'm sure he's told me dozens, if not hundreds of lies. I'm going to text Cori and tell her I'm using her as my alibi. Not that he would ask her, but he might mention something to Marcus, her husband. He does talk to him once in a while." She typed out her text and received a heart and a thumbs up in response. A moment later another text from Cori arrived. *Watch your heart with her.*

Tara considered responding to let Cori know how annoyed that made her but decided against it. She knew Cori was only looking out for her out of love. She typed out a response to Michael's text. *Having dinner with Cori. I thought I told you.*

His response was quick and simple. *You didn't.* She put her phone on silent and set it face down on the table. She had no desire to hear from him—or Cori—this evening. He could just figure out his own dinner and Cori could put her reservations about Megan somewhere else. Tara just wanted a relaxing evening with no strings attached or anything to worry about. Not that there wasn't anything to worry about with Megan. As much as she didn't want to think about it, Cori was right. She did need to watch her heart.

Chapter Eleven

I've got your affidavit all typed up and ready for you to sign," Jackson said, sliding the stapled papers across the desk to Megan. He placed a pen on top. "Take your time. Read it over and make sure everything is accurate. Go ahead and sign it if it looks good. Don't be afraid to tell me if something isn't right. This needs to be as exact as it can be."

Megan looked over at Tara before she picked up the papers. She could only imagine how hard this was for her. Yes, her own girlfriend had cheated on her. But that was much simpler. Megan moved out. She didn't have to go through all the legal stuff or deal with the woman she had cheated with.

Everything in the document was correct. She signed her name, double-checked the date on her phone, added that, and slid it back to Jackson. "All set."

He slipped the papers into a folder. "Tara, we are all set to move forward. Did you have any other questions?"

She looked up at him. "Yes. If I don't take everything when I stay at my sister's, can I go back and get it later, or is that like abandoning it or something and Michael can refuse to give it to me?"

"That is a good question. You have the right to retrieve your own property. Make me a list, you can email it to me, of any joint property that you would like to have. We will have to negotiate that with Michael and his lawyer. You said at our first meeting that you weren't going to ask for the house. Is that still the case?"

Tara nodded. "Yes. As long as I get the money from the prenup, I can get my own place."

"Understandable. I think we are all set here. Let me know if anything changes. Michael should be served on Wednesday. That gives you a few days to move to your sister's house."

"How are you doing?" Megan asked as they stepped out of the building. "Stupid question. I can see this isn't easy for you."

Tara looked at her and Megan could see her eyes starting to water. She pulled her in for a hug. "I'm so sorry."

"You have nothing to be sorry for. You have been nothing but supportive. And I appreciate it." She pulled back. "I will get through this. It's just a blip on the radar screen of my life."

"That," Megan said, "is a good attitude and quite commendable."

Tara let out a small laugh. "I've had nothing but time to come up with, what shall we call them, sayings? Slogans? Mantras? It's just a season. This too shall pass. Men suck. Okay, not all men. Just Michael."

They started walking toward the parking lot. "Yes. Michael sucks," Megan agreed. "What are you going to do now?"

"You mean right now? I'm going to go home and start packing up my clothes. Michael won't be home from work for a few hours. I think I can put some boxes in my closet so he doesn't see them. I already took the day off from work tomorrow, so I'll do the rest then. I'm thinking it will probably take a couple trips to get everything to my sister's. I'm hoping to be out of the house by tomorrow night."

"I really wish I could help you with all that. But know I'll be with you in spirit," Megan said as they reached Tara's car.

"That means more to me than you'll ever know. Thank you." She gave Megan a quick hug, got into her car, and drove off.

Megan stood on the sidewalk and watched her leave. Her heart ached for her and what she was going through. She wanted to do more to help, but knew there was nothing else she could do.

Megan didn't feel like going home. The restless feeling coursing through her was becoming a habit after she spent time with

Tara. One phone call later, she pointed her car in the direction of her sister's house.

"Hey," Jill said. "Come on in. What's going on? You sounded kind of weird on the phone."

"I'm always weird." Megan followed Jill into the kitchen, threw her coat over the back of a chair, and plopped down in it.

"True. But weird, even for you. Do you care if I start supper? Todd will be home soon, and he has his bowling league tonight, so I try to have food ready for him."

"Go right ahead. And you're right. I'm in kind of a weird mood." She propped her elbow up on the table and rested her head on it, watching her sister open a box of spaghetti and pour the contents into a pot of boiling water on the stove.

"Why? What's going on?"

"You know I told you Mike was married."

"Yes." Jill poured salt into her hand and added it to the pot.

"A lot has happened since then. Tara, that's his wife, asked me if I would help her prove he cheated. She wants to divorce him and gets a bucket load of money if there is infidelity."

Jill pulled out the chair across from Megan and sat down. "She did? That's kind of ballsy. What did you say?"

"I told her I would. I've met with her lawyer and her—twice   ”

"Twice?" Jill interrupted. "How long ago did she ask you?"

Megan filled her in on the details, including the times they'd spent together.

"Why in the hell would she invite you to go to Philadelphia, and more importantly, why would you agree to go?" Jill paused. "And why does your face light up when you talk about her?"

Megan shook her head. How could she explain having feelings for her ex-boyfriend's wife. "I like her?" It was the simple truth.

"You like her? What do you mean you like her?"

"I mean I like her. The more time I spend with her, the more I want to."

"Mike's wife? You want to spend time with Mike's wife?"

Megan let out a breath and nodded.

The expression on Jill's face went from confused to surprised. "Oh," she said. "You like her. Really like her."

"Yes."

"Does she know? I mean—I don't know what I mean. Do you know what I mean?"

Megan laughed. "The crazy thing is, I do know what you mean. You want to know if I told her."

Jill nodded.

"No. I didn't tell her. She has enough going on without her worrying about my feelings for her."

"Yeah. I can understand that. It must be frustrating for you."

"I'll survive it. She's become a good friend, and I don't want to do anything to mess that up."

Jill stood. "You're more than welcome to stay for dinner, by the way." She took two containers out of the freezer. "There's more than enough."

"Is that your homemade sauce from the tomatoes that you grew?"

"It is."

"Then I'm staying."

The sudden cry that could be heard from another room as well as the baby monitor on the counter let them know that Harper was awake from her nap. "Would you mind going to get her?" Jill asked.

"Not at all." Megan started down the hall.

"And please change her diaper," Jill called after her.

"If it's a stinky one, she's all yours," Megan called back. "Hey there, sweet girl." Harper stopped crying and gave her the biggest smile. She pulled herself up by the bars in the crib, waiting for Megan to pick her up. A quick diaper change—nothing stinky— later, and they rejoined Jill in the kitchen. Megan expected Harper to reach for her mother, but she was apparently content to sit with Megan. Megan smiled at her, and she smiled back. That was just what Megan needed.

"Do you plan on ever telling Tara how you feel?" Jill stirred the pan with the chunks of frozen tomato sauce, and the smell wafted through the kitchen, making Megan's stomach rumble.

"I'm hoping my feelings settle down and this is just a passing crush."

"What do you think the chances of that are?"

"Zero to maybe five percent," she answered. "She's not the first straight…" she let the word drift off. "She's not the first female I've had a crush on that I didn't dare tell."

Jill turned toward her, wooden spoon in hand, dripping sauce onto the stove. "She's not totally straight, is she?"

Damn it. She'd promised not to tell. She didn't answer.

"Your silence confirms it. How do you know? Did she tell you?" She put her free hand on her hip, waiting for an answer. "Wait. Does this change anything? Can you tell her how you feel when her divorce is final or at least started?"

Megan shook her head. "Probably not. I don't want to put her on the spot or make her feel uncomfortable. I don't want to risk losing her as a friend."

"What if she feels the same?"

Harper looked up at Megan and babbled. "My thoughts exactly," Megan said to her. She turned her attention to her sister. "Harper said she doesn't think Tara feels the same. She is going through hell right now. She doesn't have room for other feelings."

"That won't last forever. How about after this is all done?"

"How about you concentrate on cooking, and I pay attention to this little angel on my lap?"

"Is that your subtle way of telling me to change the subject?" Jill asked.

"Was that subtle? I thought it was pretty straightforward."

"Ass."

Megan covered Harper's ears. "Hey. Baby in the room."

Jill used her free hand to spell out A-S-S in American Sign Language.

"Yeah. As if Harper can't figure out what you're signing. Really, Jill. What kind of a mother are you?"

"She happens to be an excellent mother." Megan hadn't noticed Todd, Jill's husband, come in. He gave Jill a kiss on her cheek. Megan was happy—and a little jealous—that her sister had such a great guy. He turned to Megan and Harper. "Hi, my little cutie."

"Hi to you too," Megan said.

"I was talking to Harper, but you're kind of cute too."

"You flatter me, good sir." Megan laughed.

"Dinner's almost ready," Jill said. "Why don't you go change your clothes? Megan volunteered to set the table for us." She gave Megan a look and raised her eyebrows.

Megan put Harper in the Pack 'n Play set up in the corner, grabbed a stuffed animal that was in there, and handed it to her. "Shall I use the good china?" she asked Jill.

"I would say yes if I had good china. So you're gonna have to use the crap stuff. So sorry."

"Quite alright. I'm used to it."

"Used to what? Eating off of crap dishes? You poor baby."

"I know. I'm so deprived." Megan loved this kind of teasing banter with her sister. They'd done it forever. It used to drive their mother crazy. She didn't get their humor and wasn't amused by it.

Todd rejoined them. He pulled the high chair up to the table, retrieved Harper, and strapped her into it. She picked up the cracker he placed on the tray and took a bite.

"What do you want to drink?" he asked Megan.

"Whatever you guys are having is fine."

"Water it is." He scooped ice into three glasses and filled them with filtered water from the refrigerator.

Being with family really helped Megan lose that uneasy restlessness she felt when she watched Tara drive away from the lawyer's office earlier.

"Megan," Todd said.

She turned to him. "Yeah."

"I asked you if you wanted lemon in your water. Where ya been in there?" He pointed to her head.

"Just happy to be with you guys. It's just what I needed. And no on the lemon. Why ruin perfectly good water with something so sour?"

"Aaand she's back," Jill teased her. She set a bowl of spaghetti on the table.

Megan's mind quickly ran through a list of snappy responses, but she rejected them all. She was just happy to be there. She could think about Tara tomorrow.

Chapter Twelve

Tara unloaded the last of her things at her sister's house. She piled the boxes against the wall in the guest room. The note she left for Michael was short and not too sweet.

I need some time away from you. This isn't working for me, and I don't think it has been working for you either. I'll be staying at Anna's house for now. I'm sorry it has to be this way.
   Tara

She sat on the bed and looked at the boxes. She hadn't bothered taking any household items. She'd emailed a list of what she wanted from the house to her lawyer. She wasn't going to stress over what Michael refused to let her have.

The boxes were labeled, and she'd made sure the ones with her clothes were on top so she could unpack them before they got too wrinkled.

The clothes could wait, she decided. A glass of wine was called for, both to celebrate her newfound freedom and to settle her nerves caused by her newfound freedom. How ironic. The good and the bad were all wrapped up together.

Anna wasn't home from work yet, but Tara knew where she kept the wine glasses. She poured herself a glass from the bottle she'd brought with her. Too bad if Michael missed it. She settled herself in the living room and called Megan. She was disappointed when the phone went to voicemail. More disappointed than she thought was reasonable. She sat back and sipped her wine. It warmed her but didn't comfort her. She wasn't sure, in that moment, if anything would ever comfort her again. She knew she was being maudlin and these feelings would pass, but she felt overwhelmed by them in the moment.

She finished her wine and contemplated having another, decided against it, and went back into the guest room. She pulled the first box over to the closet and opened it. She'd packed her dresses and shirts on their hangers, so it was easy enough to hang them up. The second box was the same. She was just about to open the third box when her sister appeared at the bedroom door.

"Hi. Getting settled in?" Anna asked. "Need any help?"

Tara turned to her. "No. I've got it. Where's Brandon?"

"He always plops himself in front of the TV when he gets home. It helps him decompress from his day at school."

"That's what wine is for," Tara said with a smirk.

Anna leaned against the doorframe. "I'm afraid I would get arrested if I started giving him wine and someone found out."

"More for me, then. Don't worry about making dinner. I'm going to order food for us. In the mood for anything special?"

"I'm in the mood to see you happy."

"I'm not sure where to order that from, but I'll keep looking."

"How can I help?"

"Google search, maybe?" Tara's phone rang.

"Is that Michael?" Anna asked.

Tara's stomach went sour at the thought. "Only if he got home from work early." She retrieved the phone from the top of the dresser where she had set it earlier. Her stomach did a different kind of flip when she looked at the caller ID. "It's Megan."

"Michael's Megan?"

Her Megan now. Not Michael's. Never Michael's again. Tara closed her eyes against the thought.

"Sorry. I shouldn't have said it that way. I'll give you some privacy." She backed out of the doorway and closed the door behind her.

"Hi," Tara said into the phone.

"Hi. I'm so sorry I missed your call earlier. We were in the middle of recording."

"That's okay. I just wanted to let you know that I moved out and I'm at my sister's."

"And how are you feeling? Pretty shitty, I would imagine."

"I'm doing okay. It wasn't easy leaving the house. Leaving Michael, on the other hand, was a relief." Tara sat down on the edge of the bed.

"Does he know that you left yet?"

"I don't think so. He never gets home from work this early, and I haven't heard from him. And to be honest I'm dreading that."

"I understand. He got nasty when I broke up with him, and we'd only known each other a couple of months. Promise me that if that happens with you, you'll get a restraining order against him."

"I know he can have a temper, but he's never been violent. I don't think that would ever be a problem."

"I hope that's the case."

"How are you? How was your day?" Tara asked, changing the subject. She didn't want to think about Michael and what his reaction might be.

"It was good. The podcast went well. I think people will resonate with the subject matter. And we got a new sponsor. So, that's always good."

"What was the subject?" Just talking to Megan helped her feel calm. Peaceful.

Megan explained what she and Victoria had discussed and how well it had been researched. As much as Tara wanted to keep talking to her, she knew that if she didn't order dinner soon, they wouldn't be eating dinner until late, and while she would be fine with that, Brandon did better when his schedule was consistent. They said their good-byes and Tara reluctantly hung up.

She went in search of Anna and found her in the living room sitting on the couch with Brandon. "Chinese?" Tara asked.

"Actually, I'm part Scottish, French and English, I believe. I don't think I have any Asian in me," Anna responded.

"Just what I needed. A smart-ass answer. Would you like me to order Chinese food?"

"I'm sorry. I know you've had a hard day. I shouldn't be joking around. Yes, Chinese food would be great. Can you make sure you get sweet and sour chicken? Brandon will just eat the chicken."

"Of course. Is there a local place that you normally order from?" Tara sat in the recliner next to the couch.

"I don't know. I don't ever have food delivered."

Tara brought up the Grubhub app on her phone. She decided on a restaurant and placed the order. "Food should be here in about thirty minutes."

"I want chicken nuggets," Brandon exclaimed.

"Yep," Tara said. "I ordered chicken for you."

"Nuggets?" Brandon asked.

"Yes, nuggets," Anna said.

Tara rose. "I'm going to unpack the rest of my clothes."

"Need any help?" Anna asked.

"Nope. Thanks." Tara went back to the bedroom and closed the door. She leaned against it and covered her mouth as tears streamed down her face. She wasn't exactly sure why she was crying. Or maybe she did. She wasn't going to miss Michael. He'd left the marriage months ago. Maybe longer. Her whole life was about to be turned upside down. She'd lost her home, her security, her idea of what her future would look like. She felt displaced. Lonely. Alone.

She knew she wasn't really alone. She had her sister. She had Cori. She even had Megan. She laughed through her tears. She had Megan. Megan was the silver lining in this storm. Tara roughly wiped the tears from her cheeks. She had to get a grip, put one foot in front of the other, and do what she needed to do.

She opened the next box and set to work putting her clothes away. When she finished that she started on the box with her shoes in it. The shoes that Michael always made fun of. "Why do you need all those shoes?"

"Why did you need all these women?" she said out loud. Maybe she wasn't woman enough for him. Maybe he sensed she really didn't want a man. She didn't know, and at this point did it really matter? It didn't. She was who she was, and he had done what he had done.

Megan sent her a text later that night. It was short and simple but so appreciated. *Thinking of you and hoping you have a peaceful, restful night.* She sent a heart emoji back.

Michael still hadn't called or texted her by the time she went to bed. She wasn't sure if she was relieved or disappointed. Probably a little of both.

Despite Megan's wish, Tara's night was neither peaceful nor restful. Every time she managed to drift off to sleep, she had dreams of Michael calling her and demanding she come home. She was more tired when she got up in the morning than when she went to bed. She wished she had taken an extra day off from work.

She found Anna and Brandon in the kitchen eating breakfast after she dressed for the day. "I made you French toast." Anna pointed to the plate on the counter. "You might want to nuke them for a minute to warm them up."

"Would you be offended if I passed?"

Anna shook her head. "Do you want to take them with you for later?"

"No, thanks." Tara opened the refrigerator and retrieved the containers of leftover Chinese food from the night before. She combined several things into one container and put it in her backpack. "Where's your plastic wrap? I'll wrap the French toast up for you."

"Don't worry about it. I'll do it before I go to work."

Tara's phone pinged with a text from Megan. *Good morning. Wishing you a great day. Keep those negative thoughts at bay today. You got this!* Followed by a crazy face emoji. They were the exact words she needed today, and it brought a smile to her lips.

"Who was that from?" Anna asked. "I'm guessing from that smile on your face it wasn't from Michael."

Tara shook her head. "No. I haven't heard from him at all. It was from Megan."

"Megan? Something about your case? Must be something really good. That's the first time I've seen you smile since you got here."

"Not the case. Just wishing me a good day. She's been very supportive."

The look on Anna's face was hard to read. Confusion? Maybe. Tara didn't want to take the time to explain. She wasn't sure she could have anyway. She wasn't ready to tell her sister how she truly felt about Megan. She wasn't sure she would ever be ready. "I'm going to get going. I'm never sure after a day off from work what I'm going to find. Some of the substitutes let the kids go wild and leave messes all over the place."

"Have a good day," Anna said.

Tara appreciated the comment but realized it didn't go straight to her heart like Megan's did. It was in that moment that she understood just how much of her heart Megan held. It was both exciting and terrifying.

❖

"Thank you for inviting me for brunch today," Tara said to Megan several days later. "It's just what I needed."

"Oh, good. I figured your brain must be doing flips, considering Michael is getting served the divorce papers tomorrow. Has he been bothering you with phone calls and texts?" Megan set a container of strawberry cream cheese on the table.

"I haven't heard from him at all."

"What? You left him on Thursday, five days ago. Don't you find that strange?"

"I don't know what to think anymore. Maybe he was as relieved to be rid of me as I am of him."

"Michael is an idiot for letting someone as wonderful as you go without a fight."

The statement made Tara beam—or was she blushing? "I feel the same way about you," she confessed. "I like you. A lot. A whole lot. More than a whole lot." She wasn't sure if she should have said that or not. She'd spent so much of her life hiding who she was, it felt good to be honest.

Megan was momentarily quiet, and Tara wasn't sure what she was thinking. Maybe she'd said too much.

Megan pulled the chair out next to Tara and sat down. She reached for Tara's hand and took it in her own. The thumb she ran across the back of Tara's hand sent a surge of electricity through Tara that settled between her legs. She ignored the need to wiggle in her seat.

Megan cleared her throat and looked directly—and deeply—

into Tara's eyes. Tara felt herself tearing up with the intensity of Megan's stare.

"I feel the same. I've been too afraid to let you know. You've been going through so much."

Tara wasn't sure what to say. Her gaze fell upon Megan's lips. They looked so soft. So kissable. She knew all it would take was to lean in and she could possess those lips. She brought her eyes back up to Megan's and she could see the want—the hunger—there. It matched her own. She somehow knew she would have to make the first move, that Megan wouldn't. Just like Megan hadn't confessed her feelings until Tara did.

She leaned in and took possession of Megan's lips with her own. They were as soft as they looked. She was amazed by the reaction of her body to a kiss. She was wet, she knew that without a doubt. Every part of her body was involved in that kiss. Her toes curled in her shoes and her arms were trembling. She ran her fingers through Megan's hair and Megan pulled her in closer. Their bodies fit together like they were made for each other.

Megan lifted the edge of Tara's shirt and stroked the skin on Tara's back. A hot shiver ran through her, and Tara trembled.

Megan broke the kiss long enough to ask if she was alright.

"More than alright," Tara responded. "I've never felt like this before. It's just so…" She couldn't seem to find the words that fit.

"Right? It's just so right?" Megan offered.

Tara nodded. "But…" She paused. As much as she wanted this to go on forever. To take it to the next step, she couldn't. Not yet. She couldn't be the one that cheated.

"But we need to stop?" Megan asked.

Tara nodded again. "I don't want to. I *have* to."

Megan sat back. "I understand." She ran a single finger across Tara's cheek. Electricity shot through Tara from that gentle touch. How could a single touch cause such a reaction in her body? She grabbed Megan's hand and kissed her palm. "I'm sorry—"

Megan put a finger to her lips. "Shh. It's okay. We have time. I know you need to work some stuff out first. It's fine. It really is." She gave Tara a reassuring smile.

"Thank you," Tara said.

"No. Thank you. That was one hell of a kiss." She pushed her chair back and stood. "I better get cooking here. Not that we weren't cooking a few moments ago." She smiled again. How could anyone resist those dimples?

"Let me help," Tara said.

"You sit right there and watch me. If we don't put some space between us, I can't be held responsible for what might happen."

Tara closed her eyes against the thought of what might happen. What she really wanted to happen. Megan had crossed the kitchen by the time she opened them. She did as Megan requested and sat quietly as she watched Megan preparing food for them.

"Do you like your bagels toasted?" Megan asked.

"I like my bagels like I like my women."

"Toasted?"

"Hot." Tara responded with a smile.

How could anyone not love this woman? "Like microwaved or like my original question—toasted?" She raised her eyebrows.

"I don't think I want my women microwaved. So toasted it is."

Megan was having some trouble concentrating on what she was doing. Or trying to do. That kiss made her head swim. And more than that, Tara felt the same way she did. She would give her as much time as she needed to take care of what she needed to do to end her marriage and get her life back on track. Megan knew it took time for her to get her own feet underneath her when she left Aliza. She truly did understand.

"I'm going to have to look for an apartment at some point," Tara said. "My sister has been great, but I feel out of place there. You know? I kind of feel like I'm in the way, even though she keeps telling me I'm welcome there and can stay as long as I need. She's been great. I'm the one with the problem."

Megan popped the bagel she'd just sliced into the toaster. She turned toward Tara. "You don't have a problem. It is perfectly natural to want your own place and your own space."

"Did you stay with anyone when you left Aliza?"

"No. I just moved to a different bedroom until I found my own place."

"I've just never had to do this before. I'm embarrassed to say that I've never had to find a place to live. I went from my parents' house to Michael's. I didn't even live in the dorms when I went to college. My parents insisted that I live at home."

"Sounds more like that was your parents' problem. Not yours. Why didn't they want you to live in the dorms?"

"Probably so they could still control me. They said it was to keep me safe and to save money. Looking back, I should have applied for financial aid or taken out student loans. But I let them push me around. It took me a long time to grow up."

Megan cracked four eggs into a bowl and searched in the drawer by the stove for her whisk. "We all have our own time frames for growing up. I'm still working on it myself. I'll let you know if I ever figure it out."

Tara laughed and Megan warmed to the sound of it. She vowed to herself to make her laugh as much as possible. "Being a grown-up is a lot like sanity. It's overrated."

"Thank God. I gave up on sanity a long time ago."

"Me too. We can be insane together," Megan said. "Or do you prefer to be referred to as crazy?"

"I'm just crazy enough to be interesting. But I think sometimes I'm totally insane."

Megan looked at her for several seconds trying to figure out if she was being serious. She wasn't sure. "For real?" she finally asked.

"What? Do I think I'm insane?"

Megan shook her head. "No. I think you're very sane. Very intelligent. Very beautiful. I've thought that from the first moment I met you." She watched as a blush made its way to Tara's cheeks.

"You never said anything. About the way you felt about me, I mean."

Megan couldn't help but laugh. "And I never thought I would. You didn't either. I couldn't imagine anything happening between us. I was surprised you liked me at all considering how we met."

"I thought you were honest and kind when I met you," Tara said. "And damn cute. But yeah, I can see how you would think that. You agreed to help me when you didn't have to. Hell, you didn't even have to break up with Michael if you didn't want to. I had no way of making you do anything. You did it of your own free will. I can't thank you enough for that."

Megan found the whisk and set it on the counter. "Stop thanking me. Any decent person would be doing what I've done for you."

"Oh yeah, I left out decent when I was saying what I thought of you." She paused and seemed to think about her next words. "And Megan, I did think about you. A lot. More than I even wanted to admit to myself."

"Was it frightening? When you realized you were developing feelings for me?" Megan whisked the eggs while she waited for Tara to answer, which seemed to take forever.

"When I was younger, having feelings for other girls was frightening. The dreams I had about being with another female scared me to death. I didn't want to be gay. My parents pounded it into my head that I would go to hell if I was or even seemed like I was."

Megan poured the eggs into a frying pan and quicky stirred them around. "Do you think they knew and were trying to make sure you never acted on it?"

Tara seemed to think about it for several long moments. "Maybe. But they never wanted me to act on anything. They didn't want me to date boys either until I met Michael, and they found out he had money." She put her hand on her chin. "I was more confused than frightened about having feelings for you. I mean, I've come to terms with being gay, but being married to a man, I never thought I would act on it. Then you came along and my relationship with Michael was ending. I didn't know what to do with the feelings."

Megan turned to her. "I'm sorry if I made things hard for you."

"No. You made things clear for me. The hard part is not acting on my feelings. Not yet, anyway." Tara's cheeks turned a darker shade of red.

"Believe me, I understand. But…" She paused to make sure she had Tara's full attention. "There is no rush. We have time."

"Thank you for saying that."

"I'll make a deal with you." Megan scraped the cooked eggs into a bowl. "I'll stop apologizing if you stop thanking me." She set the bowl on the table.

"I'll do my best."

"That's all I ask." Although that wasn't all she wanted to ask.

But she knew she could wait—for as long as necessary. Tara was worth it.

Megan peered into the oven, and the smell of bacon wafted through the room. It looked like it was cooked to crispy perfection. She set the pan on top of the stove, buttered the bagels, and popped two more in the toaster. It only took a few more minutes to have everything ready and on the table. She took a seat across from Tara.

"Everything looks so good," Tara said.

Megan focused her attention on Tara and responded, "It sure does."

Chapter Thirteen

Tara was just leaving work when her phone rang. She hurried to her car before answering. She wanted to get out of the cold that was made worse by the wind. Her heart leaped to her throat when she realized it was Michael.

"Hello," she said, preparing herself for his anger.

"I got the divorce papers. We need to talk," he said.

"We can do that with our lawyers present." She tried to sound stronger than she felt.

"Yeah, we can do that later. But we need to discuss something first. It's important, Tara." She hated the sound of her name coming from his mouth. "You owe me at least that much. Meet me at the house tonight."

"Why?"

"We need to talk," he repeated. "I'm not going to fight you on the divorce, if that's what you're thinking. Tonight. Seven o'clock."

"I'll meet you, but not at the house. Meet me at Starbucks on Thorn Street."

"What? You're all of a sudden afraid to be alone with me? What do you think I'm going to do?"

Tara wasn't sure but she didn't want to find out either. "Starbucks."

"Fine. I'll be there." The line went dead, and Tara stared at her phone in disbelief. Not disbelief that Michael had demanded to meet with her. Disbelief at herself that she agreed to it, even if it was at a place of her choosing.

She wondered if she should call Megan and tell her. She decided against it. She could fill her in later if there was anything to report. She would tell her sister just so someone would know where she was and who she was meeting. She didn't really think Michael would hurt her, and hopefully being in public would stop him from berating her.

She skipped the dinner Anna made, knowing it wouldn't sit well with all the acid her stomach was producing. She'd lived with Michael for twelve years. Why would the thought of sitting across from him for what—a half hour, an hour at the most—make her so nervous?

Michael was already there when she walked in. He waved her over. "I got you a bottle of water," he said. "I know that coffee this late would mess with your sleep." He didn't sound angry like she expected.

She reluctantly sat down. The acid occupying her stomach rose up her throat.

He slid a large envelope across the table to her.

"What's this?" she asked.

"Open it. Take a look." Was that a smirk on his face?

She opened the envelope and pulled out a pile of pictures. Tara was confused. The pictures were of her. And Megan. There was a picture of her outside of Megan's apartment building on the morning they went to Philadelphia judging from the clothes she was wearing. There were pictures of the two of them together in the art museum, including a few when Tara linked her arm with Megan's. There were some from the hotel lobby and one of them just before they went into their room. "What is this?" She looked up at Michael.

"Oh wait. There's more. He pulled his phone from his shirt pocket, turned it so Tara could see it and pressed play on a video. It was Megan and her standing outside their hotel room door. "One bed." She remembered saying it. She had no idea someone had recorded it.

"How did you get these?" Her voice trembled. He obviously knew she had contacted Megan and was going to use her against him. She was still confused why he had all these pictures.

"You forgot that I'm the one who pays the cell phone bills. I also have access to any phone numbers you call. I made a call of my own and hired a private investigator to follow you." He sounded so smug.

"So, you know I called your mistress. The woman you were cheating with." At this point it probably didn't matter that he knew. All it did was take away the element of surprise.

"Oh no, baby. You've got that wrong. She's the woman you've been sleeping with."

"What are you talking about? I never slept with her."

"These pictures and especially that video tell a different story. You think you're going to get a judge to believe that you aren't personally involved with the woman you planned on using against me?"

Tara was still confused.

"You're the one that slept with her." Tara consciously tried to keep her voice low, when all she wanted to do was scream at him.

"You're not going to be able to prove anything. Even if someone saw us together, it could be because…" He put his hands together and brought them up to his lips. "Hmm. Because you convinced her to try to seduce me. Which of course didn't work." He winked.

She had the urge to leap across the table and punch him in the throat. She hadn't worried about him being violent and now she had to control her violent urges to do him harm. The bastard. How could he do this?

"So," he started. "Looks like you're the one that got caught cheating. Not me. Which means, yes, you get your divorce. But you get none of my money." He pushed his chair back, scraping it across the floor, and rose. "Enjoy your water. It's probably all you'll be able to afford soon. Oh, and you can keep the photos. I've got plenty of copies."

She could hear him laugh as he walked away. Throwing up wasn't out of the question. She made it to her car before she started crying.

The tears had mostly subsided before she attempted to drive to her sister's. They started all over again as soon as she walked in and her sister asked her what was wrong. "Did he hurt you?" she asked.

Tara shook her head. She was having trouble talking through

her sobs. Anna led her to the couch and sat her down. Brandon was nowhere to be seen, and Tara assumed he was in his room.

Anna left and returned with a glass of water and a wad of tissues, which she handed to Tara. Wiping her tears didn't stop them from flowing. It took a couple more minutes to gain enough control to tell Anna what had happened. How she'd gotten together with Megan and the friendship that had developed and now Michael planned on using that against her. She left out the part where she confessed her feelings to Megan or their kiss.

"What an ass. Do you think he stands a chance of winning?"

"I don't see why he wouldn't. If the judge thinks I got Megan to lie for me, then it's all over."

"What are the chances of finding someone else he cheated with?"

"There is no way to do that. I was lucky I found out about her. He was careful. I'll give him that. But he turned this whole thing around and made it look like I'm the one that cheated. I don't know what to do."

"I think that's a question for your lawyer."

Tara looked at the clock on wall. "I don't think I could get a hold of him now."

"I mean in the morning, or after work tomorrow. You have time to figure this out. And this Megan, she's become a real friend? I mean, you went to Philly together. I'm a little surprised at that."

Tara considered whether or not to tell Anna the whole truth. She knew she could trust her but…But what? Would Anna feel different about her if she told her the truth? She wasn't sure.

"What aren't you telling me?" Anna asked.

"What?"

"You're holding something back. Is it about this Megan woman?"

Tara just looked at her for a few seconds, trying to decide what to say.

"I'm not saying you're lying. I mean, I believe you. I'm not even sure what I'm asking."

"Yes," Tara said. "There is more. Michael is wrong. I didn't cheat. He knows that, but he'll lie or do whatever he has to do to win and not pay me what I deserve to get."

"What else is there?"

"I like Megan. I didn't expect to. Hell, I didn't want to. But I do."

"So, you became friends. What's wrong with that?"

"The feelings go beyond that," Tara said. She averted her eyes. She didn't want to see the look on Anna's face.

"Beyond what? Beyond friendship? What does…" She hesitated. "Oh. Um. Okay. Did you…?" She let the question trail off.

"No. I didn't cheat. I told you."

"But how? I mean…but how? I'm confused."

Tara dabbed at a few tears that trailed down her face and explained how she met Megan to talk about having her help and how a friendship developed and then feelings that went beyond that.

"Is she the first woman you've had feelings for?" Anna asked.

Tara shook her head. "No. I've been this way my whole life. I just never told anyone or acted on it."

"Till now?"

"I didn't cheat," Tara said a little more sternly than she intended. "Unless kissing is considered adultery."

"You kissed her?" The surprise was evident in her voice.

"It was kind of mutual and it didn't go any further. I am not a cheater. Yes, the money had something to do with it, but I'm not a cheater. I didn't want to compromise my principles."

"And how does Megan feel?"

"She feels the same way about me that I feel about her, and she seemed to understand when I stopped and said we couldn't take it any further until I'm divorced."

"So, you want to take it further?"

Oh my God, yes! "Yes. The feelings are real."

"How come you never told me?"

"I didn't want you to hate me."

"I could never hate you. That's just crazy."

"I don't know what else to say. You know Mom and Dad drilled into us how not following the rules would send us straight to hell. I know they would hate me. I wasn't sure about anyone else," Tara explained. In hindsight, thinking Anna would hate her *was* pretty stupid.

"Why on earth would you believe anything *they* told you?"

Tara shrugged. Anna had a point. "I don't know. It's stupid." Tara stood. "I'm going to go lie down. This evening has exhausted me."

"I'm sure." Anna stood and gave Tara a tight squeeze. "I love you, and nothing will ever change that."

"Ditto." Tara got ready for bed. She lay awake for she didn't know how long. Her conversation with Michael ran through her mind as well as her potential conversation with Megan. She wasn't sure how to handle that. She didn't want to hurt her, but becoming friends with her came back to bite Tara in the ass. Could she continue to see her, or would that only cause more destruction? Tara didn't know and she was terrified to find out.

Jackson suggested that Tara come into his office after work so he could see the photos Michael had given her. He gave no indication of what it might mean for her case. He didn't have to. Tara knew it would blow it out of the water.

The day seemed to drag, and Tara had a very hard time concentrating on her job. She breathed a sigh of relief after the last child had been picked up for the day. The day was dark and gloomy as she walked to her car. It seemed to fit her mood perfectly.

She had to wait fifteen minutes for Jackson while he finished up with another client. The chairs in the waiting room were less than comfortable. Tara turned down the offer of water or a cup of coffee from the secretary. Her attempt to read the outdated *People* magazine was futile. The words became a blur as her eyes filled with tears. *Damn it. Not now.* There were no tissues in sight, so she used her sleeve to dab at her cheeks.

Jackson escorted his client out and greeted Tara. "Come on in."

Tara took the seat across from the desk and handed him the envelope with the photos. Her eyes welled up again as she studied his face trying to get a clue of what he was thinking.

"If I understand this, Michael said he would use these to convince a judge that you were the one cheating?"

"Yes. But I didn't. I swear I didn't."

"Hmm. That might be hard to prove at this point. It's going to be your word against his."

"What about Megan? I haven't told her any of this yet, but if she's still willing to testify, won't that count for something?" She needed some sort of reassurance that everything would be okay.

"He can claim that she's lying too. And these pictures don't help the situation. You mentioned a video. What was on that?"

Tara told him about it.

"I'm not here to judge you, but why were you and Megan in a hotel out of town? It helps me to have all the information."

"She'd never been out of New York State. I thought it would be a nice trip. We didn't plan on spending the night, but the weather was bad, and I didn't want to drive in a snowstorm. The hotel only had one room available, so we took it."

"And nothing happened between the two of you?"

"Nothing."

"And since then?"

"What do you mean?" Tara knew exactly what he was asking but needed time to think of how to answer. She decided that the truth was the best way to proceed. "We kissed. Once. I stopped it and it didn't go any farther."

Jackson tapped his fingers on the desk and blew out a breath of air. "Hmm."

"Are we screwed?" Tara asked, afraid she already knew the answer.

"It definitely makes things harder. When exactly did you start communicating with Megan? Was there any chance it was before Michael started seeing her?"

"Absolutely not. I only called her after I found her phone number in his phone."

Jackson pulled a legal pad from his desk drawer. "Remind me what the date of that was?" He wrote down Tara's answer. "How many other times have the two of you gotten together? Dates, places, and the reason for each visit."

Tara filled him in. She realized that her feelings for Megan were pretty strong considering the number of times they'd actually seen each other, which wasn't that many in the grand scheme of things. She was surprised and at the same time not. Megan seemed to draw her in from the start.

"About how many times would you say you've talked on the phone?"

Tara pulled her phone from her purse and attempted to count the phone calls. She gave him a number. "That's as close as I can get. Michael would probably have an exact number because he can look it up on the account."

"We can see about alimony if our bid to collect on the prenup doesn't prove fruitful. I'm sure you would be granted that."

"Do you have any idea how much that would be?" Tara hadn't thought about alimony. She was so focused on the prenup. Up until last night she thought it was a sure thing.

"We have to wait to see. Michael will have to produce his financials. It will be based on several factors, especially that." He paused. "I really hate to say this, but it's my professional opinion that you should stop socializing with Megan. And no phone calls either. I don't even want you calling her to tell her any of this."

"I can't just stop talking to her without telling her why."

"I'll email her for you if that would help."

Tara nodded. Not talk to Megan? How could she do that to her? And to herself?

CHAPTER FOURTEEN

Megan hadn't heard from Tara in three days. She'd texted several times and called a couple more. She wasn't sure what to do. She had no idea where her sister lived or worked, or even her last name.

She had trouble concentrating during the recording of their latest podcast. Thank God Victoria was able to pick up the slack and keep the conversation going. "I'm sorry," she said after they wrapped. "I'm off my game today."

"What's going on?" Victoria asked after Lynn made her exit.

"I haven't heard from Tara in a few days and I'm getting worried."

"Have you tried calling her?" Victoria unplugged her microphone and loosely wrapped the cord around the stand.

"Yeah, and she doesn't answer or call me back."

"And that's unusual?"

"If we don't talk every day, we at least text. What if something's happened to her and no one knows to tell me? I'm about ready to call the hospitals to see if she's been admitted anywhere."

Victoria finished with her mic and started on Megan's. "How about her lawyer? He might know if something happened or what's going on."

Megan pointed at her. "You know, that's probably not a bad idea. Other than Michael, he's the only one that knows both of us." She stood. "Can you finish up here if I go? I can call him from my car. I don't know how long he'll be in his office." She paused. "Or if he's even there at all right now."

"Sure. Go. I got this. Good luck. Let me know how it goes."

"Thanks." Megan grabbed her coat from the back of the chair and headed out the door without putting it on. She regretted that decision as soon as she stepped outside. Not only was it getting dark, but the wind whipped the snow up in the parking lot and sent it swirling around her face. She roughly pulled the coat on and wrapped it around her, ignoring the fact that it had a zipper. She started the car and pulled her phone from her pocket. She grabbed Jackson's business card from the cup holder between the seats where she'd dropped it the day he gave it to her. She had no reason then to think she would ever need it. Now she was grateful she had it.

The phone rang long enough that Megan was about to hang up when a breathless man answered. "Jackson O'Brian law offices." She wasn't sure if it was him or someone else. He'd had a female secretary when she was there with Tara, but who knows, could have been a temp.

"This is Megan Montgomery. I'd like to speak to Mr. O'Brian if he's available."

"Megan, this is Jackson."

"Oh." She hesitated. "Sorry. I guess I didn't expect you to answer the phone yourself."

"My secretary left for the day, and I was just walking out the door. What can I do for you?"

"I haven't heard from Tara in several days. And to be honest with you, I'm worried about her. Would you happen to know if she's okay or if something happened to her?"

Jackson seemed to hesitate on the other end of the phone. "I sent you an email explaining everything."

Megan was confused. "Explaining what? I didn't get any email."

"Check your spam folder. For some reason emails from a lawyer seem to end up there. Anyway, I'm late for an appointment. Read the email. Gotta go." He hung up before Megan had a chance to reply. She found the email he was referring to in her spam folder, just like he said.

Megan,

Tara asked me to let you know that she won't be able to communicate with you for the time being. While I can't give you details, I can say there are legal reasons involving her divorce settlement. I'm sure you understand that she needs to do what is in her best interest.

Sincerely,

Jackson O'Brian

That didn't really explain anything. Megan was supposed to help Tara with her divorce settlement. Why was she being cut out and why wouldn't Tara let her know what was going on? It didn't make any sense.

"What the actual hell?" Megan said to the cold air in her car. She turned the heater on. The air that rushed at her was slightly warm. It was better than the frigid air that surrounded her. She shivered as much out of frustration and anxiety as she did from the cold. The car was considerably warmer by the time she pulled into her parking lot, and her anger was considerably stronger.

She stomped up to her apartment and was greeted by Dozer, who evidently wanted to trip her to show his affection as he weaved between her legs. "I love you too, buddy, but you gotta let me through. I've had a rough day, and you aren't helping."

He stopped his attempt to knock her off balance and jumped up on the table. It was forbidden territory, and he didn't seem to care. Today, Megan didn't care either. She wasn't sure what to do with herself. She didn't feel like doing research for their next podcast. Watching TV or a movie didn't appeal to her. Maybe a hot bath to chase away the chill that seemed to be occupying her body right down to her bones would help. "Might help the cold in my bones, but it won't help the cold in my heart," she said. "Now, that sounds like the lyrics of a country song." She threw her coat across a chair in the living room as she passed through on her way to the bathroom. She filled the tub, set her phone near enough that she could answer it if Tara called, removed her clothes, and slid into the hot water. It did help with her bones. Her heart still hurt. So many questions ran through her head, but she always came back to the same one. *Why?*

Why would Jackson tell Tara not to see or call me? And why would Tara listen to him? If nothing else she deserved an explanation.

She held her breath, slid down, and submerged her head. She wanted to block out the world and all of her feelings. The water in her ears distorted the sound of her phone ringing, and she almost dismissed it as her imagination. Almost.

She came up so fast that she splashed water on the floor that barely missed her phone. Tara's name popped up on the caller ID. She grabbed the phone with dripping wet hands, and it slid out of her grasp. Her second try was successful. She answered the phone, put it on speaker and set it on the edge of the tub. "Hello."

"First let me say I'm so sorry. I know you've called and texted and I didn't respond. I just wasn't sure what to say."

Megan closed her eyes and ran a wet hand over her face. "What does that mean?"

"Something happened with Michael the other night."

Oh my God, Megan thought. She's going back to him. "Tara, please—"

"I can explain everything. Michael had pictures. Pictures of us, Megan. Together."

"What do you mean together?"

Tara described the photos and the video to Megan. "He said it proves that I'm the one that cheated. That I got you to say you slept with him to help me."

"But he knows that isn't true."

"Of course he does. But he doesn't care. He doesn't have a problem with lying. He's lied to me. He's lied to you, and he'll lie in court. My lawyer said it would be my word against his. And he had pictures. I have you, but that won't matter if the judge believes him over me."

"Why couldn't you tell me this? Why did I have to ask your lawyer if you were okay? For God's sake, Tara, I didn't know if you were dead or alive. I was worried sick." Her voice trembled.

"I'm so sorry. You talked to Jackson? When? Did he tell you what happened? He said he would email you and tell you what was going on."

"I didn't see the email until today. I called him because I was worried about you. The email didn't tell me much. Did he call you? Isn't that why you're calling me now?"

"No. I called you because I miss you and wanted you to know what's going on. Jackson told me we shouldn't see each other. It would only give Michael more ammunition."

"And you agreed to it? Just like that? And you didn't bother telling me until now?" Megan wasn't sure if she was more hurt or angry.

"I didn't want to hurt you, and I wasn't sure how to tell you."

"And you didn't think it would hurt me if you didn't answer my calls or my texts?"

"I thought I would be able to explain. I just needed time to figure it out."

"And while you're figuring it out, I'm left blowing in the wind. Thanks a lot." Megan knew she was overreacting and only making the situation worse. She had been scared that something bad had happened to Tara and now she was scared of losing her.

"Megan, I—"

"Wait." Megan interrupted her. "We can't talk or see each other at all?"

"Jackson said not to until the divorce is settled." Tara's voice broke and Megan thought she might be on the verge of tears.

Until the divorce was settled? That could take months or even years. How could she be expected to just let Tara go like that when she had so many feelings for her? And how could Tara agree to that? It wasn't fair. She felt like she'd just been punched in the gut and had the wind knocked out of her. She needed time to think. This couldn't be the end of them. Not when it was just the beginning and held so much promise.

"Megan?" Tara said after a long pause.

"I've got to go," Megan replied. She realized she was trembling and about to start sobbing. That would only make things worse. She hit end on her phone and watched it tumble to the floor, landing with a soft thud on the bathmat. How could she do this? How could she stop seeing Tara? And how could she possibly stop thinking about her or wanting her?

❖

Tara stared at her phone. She'd finally gotten the nerve to call Megan and explain, and Megan hung up on her before she had a chance to tell her how sorry she was. Didn't Megan realize how hard this was for her? Obviously not. She considered calling her back but decided against it. She'd explained why she disappeared and she needed to stay away from her. Calling back wouldn't serve any purpose.

Tara couldn't believe how much she missed her, and hearing her voice only made it harder. She had expected Megan to be disappointed, but judging by the way she ended the phone call, it was much more than that.

She wasn't sure what to think—or feel anymore. It was all so unfair. She hadn't done anything wrong, yet Michael was trying to screw her out of the money she deserved, and Megan seemed mad at her.

There was a knock on the bedroom door. "Come in."

"I wasn't sure if you were off the phone. I warmed up some coffee cake for dessert. Thought you might like some before Brandon eats it all," Anna said.

"I appreciate it. Don't think my stomach would appreciate it."

"Phone call to Megan didn't go so good?" Anna asked.

"Nope."

"Want to talk about it?"

"Nope. But I'll come and sit with you while you have dessert." She slipped her phone into her pocket and followed Anna to the kitchen where Brandon was helping himself to another piece of coffee cake.

"Hey, mister," Anna said. "That is your third piece. No more after that."

He nodded at her and scooped a large bite into his mouth.

Tara pulled out a chair and sat. "She barely spoke to me."

Anna poured milk into a glass and set it in front of Brandon. "Who? Megan?"

"Yes."

"Why? You're just doing what your lawyer told you, and all of this is because of Michael, not you."

"I tried to—" Tara's phone rang in her pocket. It wasn't Megan calling her back as she had hoped. "It's Jackson, my lawyer," she said. "I'll take it in the other room."

"Hello," she said as soon as she was out of earshot.

"Hi, Tara. It's Jackson. I just wanted to let you know that Megan called me because she hadn't heard from you and apparently didn't read my email. I just wanted you to know."

"I talked to her already," Tara said. "What did she say to you?"

"You did? Oh, okay. She said she was worried about you. I'm sorry, Tara. I stand by my suggestion to keep your distance."

"Would it be a problem if I talked to her from my sister's phone or got my own phone plan? I mean, that way Michael can't track the call."

"The problem with that is if the judge asks you about your contact with her, you'll have to tell the truth. It's just until this is settled, and it's for your own financial good."

Tara reluctantly agreed. "What kind of a time frame are we looking at here? I would like to get this over with as soon as possible."

"I understand. I'll make some phone calls tomorrow and see when we can meet with Michael and his lawyer to see if we can come to an agreement without going to court. I'll be in touch."

"Thanks, Jackson."

Brandon had finished his food and was arguing with Anna when Tara returned to the kitchen.

"You are going to get a stomachache if you eat any more," Anna said. "Go get yourself ready for bed and don't forget to brush your teeth."

Brandon reluctantly left the table and headed down the hall.

"I love him, but geez he is a handful sometimes," Anna whispered. "What did your lawyer say?"

"Megan called him because she was worried about me. I don't blame her for that. We went from talking or texting every day to me not responding at all. Anyway, he is going to try to get a meeting set up with Michael and his lawyer. As much as I want this over with, I dread this part of it."

"I can understand that. I can go with you if that would help."

"I don't think that's necessary." Her sister had been so generous and loving. She didn't need to be subjected to Michael's lies or the whole ugly process of this divorce.

"Okay. Let me know if you change your mind."

She would figure this out on her own. Not only did she need to get this divorce over with, she needed to figure out how to get Megan to understand that this was just temporary and her feelings hadn't changed. She prayed she didn't do any lasting damage to their budding relationship.

❖

Tara didn't hear from Jackson for four more days. "I have a meeting set up for Wednesday. Can you come in tomorrow so we can go over everything?"

"Yes." They set up a time after Tara was done with work. They went over everything Tara wanted to get out of the divorce, the documents she'd given Jackson, and Megan's affidavit.

"And we don't need Megan there?" Tara asked.

"Not to begin with. If it goes to court, we will probably need her to testify."

Tara hoped she would still be willing to do that. She wasn't sure anymore. She wasn't sure about anything.

The meeting was quick, and Tara was grateful for that. She felt as prepared as she could be for the meeting with Michael and his lawyer. But that didn't stop the dread she was feeling.

Michael had a smug look on his face and Tara had the urge to slap it off as she sat across from him the next day. Her lawyer did most of the talking. Michael refused to honor the prenup and fought them on the amount of alimony they requested.

"You have our figures," Jackson said as they wrapped things up.

"And you have our counteroffers. Discuss it with your client and get back to me. Otherwise, we'll see you in court."

Tara watched as Michael and his lawyer left the room. "What do you think?" Jackson asked once they were alone. "It's enough to live on."

"It's not enough to help my sister," Tara responded. "And that's important to me."

"Those pictures are very damning. Even if the story Michael is telling isn't true. A judge could rule either way."

"Could a judge grant me more alimony?"

"Yes. He would look at both of your financial reports. Michael makes much more money than you do. The formula they use to figure this out is a lot more than what they offered. Michael's lawyer knows that. We can probably get him to up the amount without going to court. And they didn't even give us a chance to discuss the house."

Tara didn't care about the house and wasn't sure what Jackson was referring to. "And the money he has from his inheritance?"

"That would be up to the judge as to whether or not that could be considered. Most of it is tied up in investments, so even if it was considered it would take time to liquidate it."

"Are you telling me we're screwed?" Tara asked.

Jackson put the paperwork that was spread out on the table back into his briefcase. "Not at all. We'll work on a counteroffer. One that is satisfying to you and hopefully agreeable to them. How does that sound?"

She was still so angry about being manipulated by lies. "Whatever we have to do, I guess." She stood.

"Alright. Let me work with some numbers, now that I have all of Michael's financial information. I'll give you a call tomorrow with the new figures."

They wrapped up their conversation and Tara drove to her sister's house. Her thoughts circled around her head in a never-ending loop. She was ready to scream by the time she walked through the door.

"Judging by the look on your face I would say it didn't go well," Anna said.

Tara shook her head. "No. They wouldn't agree to anything we asked for."

"What's the next step?"

Tara hung her coat up and followed Anna into the kitchen. "My next step is making myself a cup of tea. Do you want one?"

"No, thanks."

Tara lifted the tea kettle on the stove to make sure there was enough water in it and turned on the burner under it. "My lawyer's next step is to go over Michael's financial statements again and come up with a new offer to see if they'll settle."

"Does he think they will?"

"I don't know. He says if we go to court, I can get more alimony than they are offering." Tara went on to explain the gist of the meeting. "Michael just sat there with an arrogant look on his face like he'd already won. You know what is crazy about today?"

"It all sounds kind of crazy to me," Anna said.

"I kept wishing Megan was there with me." She shook her head. She knew how insane that sounded.

"You really miss her?"

"I do. I really, really do."

CHAPTER FIFTEEN

Megan did her best to keep herself busy and to keep her thoughts from settling on Tara. She was the last person Megan wanted to think about. Her efforts were only semi-successful. She seemed to walk through Megan's mind on a regular basis. The hurt and the fear of losing her boiled up every time she made an appearance.

The dream she'd had of kissing Tara left her aroused when she woke up and scared when she realized that she might never talk to her again. She was angry at herself for getting her hopes up that she and Tara had a future together.

"How stupid can I be?" she asked Dozer. "Don't bother answering that. The answer is very." She poured fresh food into his bowl and refilled his water dish. "I'm heading to Jill's. Don't be crazy while I'm gone." She thought back to her conversation with Tara about being crazy. *There I go again. Thinking about her.*

A quick stop at the bakery around the corner for a box of cookies and another stop at the liquor store for a bottle of vodka, and she pointed her car in the direction of her sister's house. It was Todd's bowling night, and Harper would be down for the evening.

"I've got the goodies," she said when Jill answered the door. "Cookies and vodka."

"Good. I've got orange and cranberry juice." Jill hung her coat in the closet. "If you have more than two drinks, you're spending the night in the guest room. I already put out a pair of sweatpants and a T-shirt for you to sleep in."

"How do you know how much I'm going to drink?"

In the kitchen, Jill retrieved two glasses and opened the refrigerator. "Because I know you, and from the sound of your voice on the phone, you need an evening of talking and drinking." She looked at Megan. "And maybe some crying."

"I'm not crying. You're crying."

"Lame. Do you want orange or cranberry?"

"Let's live dangerously. Both."

"No," Jill said. "That's gross. You're getting orange. I have more of that."

"I'm glad that's settled."

Jill made them both a drink and headed toward the living room. "Bring the box of cookies." They settled down across from each other. "Talk to me," Jill said.

"What do you want to talk about? How's Harper?"

"She's fine. How are you?"

Megan shook her head. "I've been dumped." She took a healthy swig of her drink. It was stronger than she would have made it, but she wasn't about to complain.

"Dumped? By who? I didn't know you were seeing anyone since Mike."

"Tara dumped me." Another swig and a cookie chaser to kill some of the alcohol taste.

"I'm confused here. I know you liked her, but…" She paused. "Did she stop talking to you? You helped her and now she doesn't need you?"

"Not exactly. Her lawyer told her to stop seeing me or even talking to me."

"Come on," Jill said. "This is like pulling teeth. Stop giving me bits and pieces and tell me the whole story."

Megan filled her in on everything that had happened. She managed to keep the tears at bay until she got to the end. "So, she didn't tell me for three days what was going on. That hurts, and not seeing her hurts even more."

Jill grabbed the box of tissues next to her and tossed them to Megan. "Of course it does."

"I'm doing my best to get her out of my head."

"And how is that going?"

"Not great. The bigger problem is trying to get her out of my heart. I really care for her, Jill."

"Even now?"

Megan wiped her eyes. "Yes. That's how deeply she's entrenched there. I had such high hopes."

"And?"

"And what?" Megan took another sip of her drink and realized she'd almost finished it.

"Do you still have high hopes?"

"How can I? She won't even talk to me."

"Can't. She *can't* talk to you. There's a difference," Jill said.

Megan wasn't ready to hear logic. She wanted to be mad. At least for a little while longer.

"Earth to Megan. Are you listening to me?"

"I need another drink." Megan left Jill and her opinions, no matter how much sense they made, in the living room while she made herself another screwdriver. She returned to find Jill had disappeared. *Much like Tara did.* Except she knew Jill would be back. She wasn't so sure about Tara. She wasn't sure she wanted her to come back. Who was she kidding? Of course she wanted her to.

"Did you make me another one?" Jill asked when she returned.

"You didn't ask me to." Megan started to get up, but Jill stopped her.

"I'll get it." She grabbed her glass and headed toward the kitchen.

"Alone again. Naturally. Isn't there a song like that?" She turned in the direction Jill had headed and yelled, "Isn't there a song about being alone?"

Jill stuck her head out through the kitchen doorway long enough to put her finger to her lips.

"Oh," Megan whispered. "Harper's sleeping. Sorry."

"Or is it alone again, unnaturally?" She sipped her drink. This time it was much more to her liking—more orange juice, less vodka than the one Jill had made. "No, that doesn't make sense."

"What doesn't make sense? And don't yell when the baby's sleeping. I couldn't understand what you were saying anyway."

"I was just trying to figure out the lyrics to a song about being alone."

"You aren't alone. You know that. You've got me and Dad, Victoria, your producer friend, what's her name, and a handful of other friends that you've probably been neglecting."

She was right about that one. She hadn't felt too social lately. And before lately, she only wanted to hang out with Tara. There she was again, occupying space in Megan's mind. She had a lot of nerve showing up there so often.

"And you have Dozer. Don't forget about him."

"Never. I would never forget about him. He's my buddy. My very destructive buddy."

Turned out Tara was a destructive buddy too. Look at how easily she put a big dent in Megan's heart.

"I don't know," Tara said to Cori. "I haven't heard from Jackson yet. He presented Michael's lawyers with the new figures. As far as I know, they haven't gotten back to him."

Cori poured wine into two glasses and handed one to Tara. "Let's go sit in the family room. I started a fire in the fireplace. It's exactly what we need on this frigid night: good friends, good wine, and a warm fire."

Tara settled on the couch and pulled her feet up under her. Cori was right. This was what she needed. She was glad it was just the two of them. Not that she didn't like Cori's husband, but she needed some girl time.

Cori set the bottle of wine on the end table and settled next to Tara. "No matter what happens, you're going to get through this."

"I know. But the process is so hard. Fighting over money. It's not something I ever thought I would do. But I feel like I have to. You know? For Anna. And for Brandon."

"So, worst-case scenario, you get enough money to start over and Brandon has to go back to public school. Is that the end of the world?" She didn't wait for Tara to respond. "I mean, he'll be in high school next year. It's a whole different world than middle school."

Tara hadn't thought of that. "Anna said not to worry about it, but I do."

"You need to stop," Cori said. "You need to take care of yourself now. Stop worrying about everyone else."

"Easier said than done. I've worried about Anna her whole life. It's hard to shut it off."

"She is a grown woman with a kid of her own. I know she's had some hard times, losing her husband and raising a kid on the spectrum alone. But she can handle it. Give her some credit."

Tara was quiet while she absorbed what Cori had said. "I seem to be messing things up lately." She took a sip of her wine.

"What does that mean?"

"Michael has those pictures because of me. Brandon might have to leave his private school because of me. Megan probably hates me. Because of me."

"Now what does that mean? The Megan part." Cori set her wine on the coffee table and leaned forward.

"Jackson told me to cut off all communication with her, and I did. Only I waited three days before I told her."

"And why would that make her hate you?" she asked.

"Because I ignored her phone calls and texts during those three days. She ended up calling Jackson because she was worried about me."

Cori grabbed a couple of crackers from the plate on the coffee table and sandwiched a piece of cheese between them. "That just shows how much she cares about you."

"And I care about her. So much. I shouldn't have waited to tell her. I had no idea what to say or how to say it. I knew it would hurt her. I ended up hurting her even more by not telling her as soon as Jackson told me. I'm so stupid. How could I have done that?"

"First of all, you aren't stupid. Stop saying that. And if you didn't know what to tell her, you didn't know. I can understand you needing time to figure it out."

"Yeah. Well, Megan obviously didn't feel that way."

"Have you talked to her since?" Cori helped herself to another piece of cheese. She pushed the plate closer to Tara.

Tara put up her hand and shook her head. She'd hardly eaten a thing in the past week. And what she did eat didn't sit well in her stomach. "No. I'm following Jackson's orders."

"So, he *ordered* you to do it? Cut her off? Totally?"

Tara thought about it for a few moments. "I don't think legally he can order me to do anything. He told me that's what I should do. And I did it. It's not like I wanted to. I didn't." It hurt her heart to do it.

"Why can't you talk to her? Seems to me the damage is already done."

"He said we shouldn't give them more ammunition, basically. I assume he knows what he's doing." *Although I'm not sure what I'm doing.* "I miss her, Cori. I know we haven't known each other that long. And we met under—let's call it weird—circumstances. But she's come to mean a lot to me."

"Weird circumstances to say the least. What are you going to do?"

"I'm going to do what Jackson said. As much as it sucks." Was there any other way do this? She didn't think so.

CHAPTER SIXTEEN

The call from Jackson came just as Tara was putting the last of the small chairs on top of the round tables in her class. It wasn't mandatory, but she knew it made it easier for the night cleaning crew.

She blew out a breath before answering. "Hello."

"Tara?"

"Yes."

"It's Jackson. I've got the new figures to offer Michael. Do you want to come into the office, and we can go over them for your approval or to see if there is anything you want to change?"

Tara hesitated. She was so sick of this whole process already, and they didn't appear to be even close to a settlement.

"Or I can email them to you," Jackson continued.

"I would really appreciate that." She grabbed her jacket from the small coat closet, gave the classroom one final look, and turned off the lights.

"Great. I'll do that right now. Look them over. Email me with any changes you want or give me a call if that will be easier. I've got a pretty full day tomorrow, court and meetings, but I can get back to you if you leave a message."

Email seemed so much easier to Tara at that moment. "Okay. Thanks." She hung up the phone and slipped it into her pocket.

The winter wind greeted her with an icy blast as she stepped out the door, and she attempted to zip her jacket, which seemed to want to put up a fight. She gave up just as she approached her car. She slid into the driver's seat, fished her key from the bottom of her purse, after what seemed like several minutes of searching, and attempted to start the car. Nothing. No sound. The motor didn't turn over. "Damn it." She slammed her hands into the steering wheel and was immediately sorry. Freezing cold hands against a freezing cold steering wheel sent a bolt of pain through her right hand that traveled up to her elbow. "Shit. Shit. Shit." Banging her head against the steering wheel—her next thought—probably wasn't a good idea either.

She closed her eyes against the tears that were building up, but it didn't stop them from cascading down her cheeks. It only took a few seconds more for her to sob uncontrollably. So much seemed to be happening at once. The divorce. Moving out of her home. Losing all contact with Megan. And now her jacket and her car were plotting against her. The tears were for Megan than anything else. Everything else was fixable. She wasn't so sure about that one.

Most of the contents of the glove compartment ended up on the passenger seat as Tara searched for something to wipe her tears and blow her nose. She found a small packet of tissues with the logo from some bank that she'd been handed when she went to the county fair with Michael God knows how long ago. She'd forgotten she even had it. The package was empty by the time she got the crying under control.

She shivered, as much from her emotions as from the cold enveloping the car. Anna and Cori would still be at work. She sure as hell couldn't—wouldn't—call Michael. It was Megan she wanted to call. Who the hell was she kidding? It was Megan she wanted to see. Having car trouble was just an excuse. She wasn't even sure if Megan would help her. Did she dare call her?

The knock on her window made her jump. For a moment, she was surprised the window didn't roll down when she pressed the button, forgetting the car battery was obviously dead. At least she thought that's what the problem was.

Daniel Jones, the school principal, knocked again. "Do you need help?" he asked her through the closed window. His shoulders were hunched around his neck, from the cold Tara presumed.

Tara opened the door, and a gust of wind rushed at her. "My car won't start. Would you happen to have jumper cable thingies?" Her face was starting to go numb from the cold air on her wet cheeks. She brushed away the remaining tears.

"I don't. Why don't you come in and we'll see who we can call for help?"

Her jacket zipper refused to budge as she attempted to zip it one more time before getting out of the car. She did her best to pull it closed around her as she followed Daniel back into the school.

The hallway was quiet as they made their way to the office. Daniel unlocked the door and turned on the lights. He had obviously been on his way to his car when he spotted Tara. He sat behind his old wooden desk and motioned for Tara to take a seat across from him. He slid a box of Kleenex to her. She was sure she must have looked awful—red nose, tear-streaked mascara, hair messed up by the wind.

She attempted to wipe under her eyes to catch any smudges and a few tears, surprised she had any left.

"I'm sure you can get your car started with a jump. Sometimes when it gets this cold it affects the battery. And…" Daniel paused. "Anything you want to talk about? I mean, that's quite the reaction for a just a car problem."

Tara shook her head. "No. Just a lot going on. I'll get through it."

"I know you will. Now, where can we get some jumper cables? Is there anyone you can call? Do you have Triple A?"

"No. I mean, anyone I can think of is working."

"Parents? Is your dad retired? Maybe he could help?"

Her dad? She hadn't seen him in months. She didn't want to see him now. Did she have a choice?

"Tara?"

"Is there anyone you could call? I mean, I don't want to impose, but…"

"Unfortunately, no." He looked at his watch. "I need to get home soon and pick up my wife. We have a flight to Naples, Florida, that we can't miss. Taking a couple extra days off before Thanksgiving."

"Oh. Yes. Sorry. Um. Yeah." Was she making any sense?

"Yeah. I'll call my father. He always had jumper cables in his truck. I don't want to keep you."

Daniel stood. "Good idea. You can stay warm in my office until he gets here. Just turn off the lights and lock the door when you leave." He started for the door and turned back to her. "Happy Thanksgiving. Enjoy your holiday." He was gone before she had a chance to respond.

Thanksgiving? How had she forgotten that it was almost Thanksgiving? She hadn't even done anything with the kids for the holiday yet. She usually helped them make turkey drawings from their handprints for their parents. She'd been so lost in her own grief that she hadn't planned anything this year. She would figure it out when she got home. *If* she got home.

She considered her options. Wait for Cori or Anna to get done with work? Of course Anna had to pick up Brandon before she went home. And Tara knew that changes in Brandon's routine sometimes threw him off.

Cori was her best bet. Sometimes she could answer while she was working and sometimes she couldn't. "Hello," she said before the second ring.

"Hey. It's me. I'm stuck at work. My car won't start. I don't know if I left the headlights on or what. Any chance you can help me jump start it after work?"

"Oh wow. I wish I could. My car's in the shop and Marcus is picking me up. We're supposed to go to his parents' for dinner and then all of us have tickets to that new play at the Rochester Theater. I can cancel and get Marcus to help."

"No. No, don't do that. I'll figure something out."

"You can take an Uber home."

"I don't want to leave my car here. That would strand me, and I'd still have to figure out how to get it started. Thanks. Enjoy your evening."

How many more options did she have? Megan was definitely out of the question. Just the thought of Megan made her heart ping and hurt at the same time.

Did she dare call her father? She hadn't spoken to either of her parents in quite a while. Walking the six miles home in the freezing cold with a coat that wouldn't zip seemed like a much more appealing choice. She sat rolling the slim options around in her mind until it started to get dark.

"Crap." She pulled up her parents' contact and called them. They refused to move into the twenty-first century and still had a landline on the wall in the kitchen. They didn't even have an answering machine or caller ID.

"Hello." The sound of her mother's voice sent a cold chill through her. She hung up the phone. No. She couldn't do it.

Her phone ringing in her hand startled her and she almost dropped it. Her first thought was it was her mother calling her back—which was ridiculous. Her mother wouldn't have known it was her calling. It was Anna. Tara sighed. "Hello?"

"Hey there. I just got home with Brandon. You usually beat me home. I'm about to make supper and wanted to know if you would be home soon."

How long had she been sitting in the school office? She'd lost all track of time. "I'm stranded at school. My car won't start. I hate to ask you, but can you possibly get your hands on a jumper cable?"

"Um. Yeah. Let me get Brandon in gear and we'll find one somewhere and be there."

"Text me when you get here. I'm inside."

"Okay. See you soon."

It took Anna almost thirty minutes to arrive. Tara tried three more times to get her coat zipped without any luck. She pulled the coat around her and headed back outside into the cold.

"You don't call me when you need help?" The sound of her father's voice was like fingernails scraping a chalkboard mixed with the sound of a screech owl.

Anna shrugged and gave her an apologetic look. "Dad was the only one I could find that had jumper cables."

He opened the trunk of Anna's car and retrieved a set of jumper cables. "What? Too high and mighty for me? Is that why you called your sister instead of your own father?" She knew he wasn't joking.

"I didn't want to bother you," Tara said to her father.

"It's not like you didn't bother me while you were growing up.

Get in the car and pop the hood. And for God's sake, zip that coat up. What are you? Five years old?"

Tara climbed into the car, glad to be out of the wind. The sound of her father bitching under his breath was almost more than she could take.

"Turn the key," he said after hooking everything up.

The car started on the first try. Tara rolled down her window a couple of inches. "Thank you."

"Don't run the heater on your way home. And how come Michael didn't come to help you? I gave him jumper cables for Christmas years ago."

No. She hadn't told her parents that she had left him. She didn't plan to now.

"I couldn't get ahold of him."

"We'll follow you home," her father said. "Just in case your car quits again. Then Anna can bring me home." He waved a bony finger at her. "Don't let shit like this happen again. Get that battery checked out."

Tara rolled up the window. Damn it. Why did Anna have to call him? Wasn't there anyone else she knew with jumper cables? She backed out of the parking space and pointed her car in the direction of home. Only it wasn't her home anymore. It would only raise more questions if she drove to Anna's house.

Michael's car wasn't in the driveway, but that didn't surprise her. She was sure he was out with a new girlfriend or on the prowl looking for one. She knew his car wasn't in the garage with the way the snow was piled against it. How often had he complained that the guy he hired did a shitty job, yet he was too lazy to find someone else.

Tara was relieved to see her sister drive past and not pull into the driveway behind her. Anna's taillights disappeared as she turned the corner at the end of the street and Tara backed out onto the street. The last thing she needed was for Michael to come home while she was there.

"I'm so sorry," Anna said when she walked into the house, followed closely by Brandon, who continued down the hall to his room. "I called to borrow the cables, and he insisted on coming with me. I couldn't talk him out of it."

"Probably didn't trust us to do it without him," Tara said.

"Those were his exact words."

"Of course they were. I don't want to sound ungrateful, but God, he makes me so crazy."

"I know. I couldn't think what else to do."

"It isn't your fault. I'm just grateful we got it started. I drove it around to make sure the battery was charged. I'm surprised I got home so much before you."

"Mom snagged me and Brandon and practically dragged us into the house. She said I looked pale and thin and insisted I bring home some *decent* food." Anna held up a bag.

"My turn to say I'm sorry. Did she talk to Brandon?"

"Nope. She never does. I think he prefers it that way. He doesn't like her any more than we do."

As if on cue, Brandon came into the room. "I'm hungry."

"Brandon, I'm sorry you had to go out on such a cold night. But thanks for coming with your mom to help me," Tara said.

"It's okay," he replied.

"Go wash up, buddy. I'll get supper ready." Anna turned to Tara. "Should we eat Mom's food, or should I throw it out? You don't think she would try to poison us, do you?"

"She wouldn't poison you and she doesn't know I'm here, so it's probably safe."

Anna laughed. "I know it's not funny. But it is. Funny. And sad."

"Mom," Brandon said. "I'm still hungry."

"That makes sense seeing I haven't fed you yet. Go wash your hands and we'll eat in a few minutes."

As she lay in bed that night, so many thoughts went through Tara's head. Her father's mean words echoed until she told them to stop. Thoughts of Megan hurt too much, so she pushed them aside. When Michael popped into her head, she thought of how it started out and how badly it had ended. She grabbed her phone from the nightstand and jotted down the poem that was running through her head.

A good husband you were not
I cried and cried and cried a lot

You hurt me and you left me blue
It's not my fault, it was all you

You were so stupid and conniving
Next time I run into you
I hope I'm driving

She couldn't help but laugh at how stupid it was but how accurate it was at the same time. Yes. She was done with Michael, and things with Megan got messed up before they ever really began. There was a problem with that. She was done letting Michael take things from her. She would be damned if Michael was going to take Megan away from her too. She just needed to figure out how to change that.

CHAPTER SEVENTEEN

Tara didn't get much sleep. Her dreams circled around Megan and what could have been and what Tara was determined to explore again. She called Jackson before she was even dressed for the day. The answering machine picked up announcing that no one was in the office at the moment and to leave a message, which she did.

"What's going on?" Anna asked when Tara joined her and Brandon in the kitchen. "I thought I heard you singing in the shower." She flipped a pancake in the pan. "Breakfast?"

"I made a decision last night."

"Sit. What kind of decision?"

"No time. I need to get to work. I need to prepare a Thanksgiving project for the kids. But I need to know that you'll be okay if I can't help as much to pay for Brandon's school. I mean, I'll help as much as I can, but I don't know how much that will be." She looked down at her hands, pretty sure she knew Anna's answer, but not positive.

"I've already told you that we will be fine. Stop worrying about us. Do what you need to do for you. You deserve the life you want. I love you and appreciate what you've done so far. But please…" She paused. "Look at me."

Tara looked up.

"Please, Tara, do what's best for *you*."

Relief flooded through her. "Thank you. I love you too." Turning to Brandon, she added. "You too, big guy." She grabbed her coat on the way out the door, remembered the broken zipper, and shrugged it off. Nothing was going to get her down today. At least she hoped nothing would.

To her relief, the car started without a problem and her trip to work was uneventful. She gathered construction paper, crayons and various other supplies, and placed them on one of the small round tables in the center of the room. She was just finishing up when her phone rang. She fished it out of her desk drawer. It was Jackson.

"I called because I want you to settle. Get me as much as you can, but settle so we don't have to go to court."

"Why the change of heart? We can do much more with the threat of court hanging over their heads."

"You can threaten whatever you want to get this taken care of. I'm not cutting Megan out of my life. I mean, don't tell them that, but I'm done fighting for money and I'm ready to fight for her. The longer I wait—well—I'm afraid I might have waited too long already. I want her in my life."

"Are you sure about this? My advice—"

"I know your advice. But this is my life, and I want to live it the way I want. I've lived too much of my life for other people." She paused. "Too much information. I know. But get whatever you can get. As much as I want to stick it to Michael, there is more to life than that."

"Okay. If you're sure. Do you want me to let you know—"

"I just want to know the final figures and where to sign to get the divorce over with."

"Tara, this isn't the best—"

"It's what's best for me. Thank you. Let me know when it's settled." She hung up the phone before he had a chance to respond. She knew it was his job to look out for her best interests financially. But her best interests—the best interest of her heart had nothing to do with money.

There was still at least fifteen minutes left before the students would arrive. She sent a text to Megan. *Can we get together. There is something I would like to share with you. Please.*

❖

Megan closed her laptop. That was enough research for the morning. She'd gotten an early start—just as she'd done every day since the crap with Tara. Her sleep was less than ideal and rising early was becoming a habit—a habit she didn't like.

Dozer rubbed against her legs. "One of these days I'm going to end up on the floor from the way you show me your affection." She poured fresh food in his bowl even though it was still half full. He leaped on it as if he was starving. "Are you telling me you pretended to love me just to get more food?" She shook her head. "Of course you did. Story of my life. Pretend to like me to get what you want." She thought about that for a few moments. "Okay," she continued. "I don't think she was using me, but when push came to shove, she shoved me out of the way. Not nice."

Her phone pinged with a text from Lynn. *I emailed you some updated notes for today's show. Look it over. See you later.*

Megan made herself a ham and cheese sandwich and poured herself a glass of Mountain Dew. She wasn't big into sodas but found she needed the extra boost of caffeine to make it through the day when sleep was so elusive.

She set the sandwich on the couch next to her and opened the email on her computer. Most of the notes were arranged in neat bullet points—Megan wouldn't expect anything less from Lynn. Most of the bullet points were about the show. The last one was not. Megan read it out loud.

"I don't know what's going on with you, but you have been so off your game that I'm starting to worry. What can I do to help? This is so unlike you." Shit. She hadn't realized her internal struggles were affecting her work. She was surprised Victoria hadn't said anything. She'd never been one to shy away from calling Megan out.

What exactly had she been doing or not doing that Lynn had noticed? She wasn't sure. A quick phone call to Lynn was in order. "Got your notes. Can I ask what you mean when you say I'm off my game? Off my game how?"

"You seem like you're distracted," Lynn started. "You aren't responding to whatever Victoria says. You just say whatever the next point is as if you were reading a script. That's not like you. You are usually so engaged in the conversation. Anything you want to talk about?"

Other than her sister, she really hadn't mentioned any of this to anyone else. She spilled it all to Lynn over the phone. Lynn was quiet until Megan finished.

"That is quite the story. If it wasn't so personal, I would suggest we use it on the podcast."

"Lynn, we can't use—"

"I know. I was just saying it was an interesting topic. You got quite close to this woman in what seems like a very short amount of time."

Megan couldn't argue that point. "We did. *I did.* Apparently, I misread her feelings."

"Maybe not. Sounds like she was put in a very hard situation."

"Don't make excuses for her," Megan said.

"I'm not. What she did sucks, and it hurt you. Maybe even more than you realize. What were you expecting from her?"

"Not this. That's for sure. Not to be tossed away after she got what she wanted from me."

"Do you think she kissed you to try to get you to help her?"

"I had already helped her by that point." Megan rose and brought her sandwich back to the kitchen. She grabbed a couple of cookies from the cupboard instead.

"Then why do you think she kissed you and said she had feelings for you?"

"Damned if I know." She poured herself a glass of milk and returned to the living room.

"That's bullshit and you know it."

Megan was at a loss for words. She stuffed half a cookie into her mouth and chewed, not really tasting it.

"Nothing to say?" Lynn asked.

"I'm thinking," Megan said as a few cookie crumbs fell onto her lap. "Why is it bullshit?"

"Because she wasn't using you, which means she likes you."

"Like likes me?" Megan recalled the conversation she had with Tara in the hotel room.

"What are you? Twelve?"

I know you are, but what am I? Megan thought, proving Lynn's point about her being immature. "Okay, I get it, but she didn't have to do things the way she did."

"I'm not arguing that point. I'm not trying to argue at all. Just want to help you get your feet back under you."

She was right about that. Tara did manage to knock Megan to the ground. She'd been struggling to get back up. She wasn't sure this conversation was helping. "I'll do better today. I didn't realize I was sleepwalking through the podcasts. But now I do." She took another large bite of the cookie and drank a gulp of milk to wash it down.

"That simple, huh?"

"That simple. I wasn't aware I was doing that. Now I am. Problem solved."

"Work problem maybe. Not your own personal problem with this," Lynn said.

"That part takes time. What's the saying? Time wounds all heels." She ran the back of her hand across her mouth to wipe away the milk from her lips. The lips that had been so connected to Tara's lips not all that long ago. The lips that longed for Tara's lips again.

"You got that backward."

"No, I didn't. Think about it."

It was several seconds before Lynn replied. "Which one of you is the heel? You or Tara?"

"Maybe both of us. Or Mike. He's the biggest heel of all." Megan was tiring of the conversation. It felt like they were going around in circles. "I'll do better at work," Megan repeated. "Sorry for messing up. I'm gonna get going. I have a few errands to run before work. I'll see you later."

"Okay," Lynn said. "I didn't mean to upset you."

"You didn't. Just got a busy day. Later." Megan hit the end button on her phone. What did Lynn know? She'd been happily married, forever and her wife treated her like a queen. She'd never had to deal with people like Mike or Tara.

Her phone pinged with a text as she poured her second glass of milk. She was surprised it was from Tara. *Can we get together. There is something I would like to share with you. Please.*

The text was forgotten when Dozer jumped up on the coffee table and knocked over what was left in the glass. Megan watched it happen as if it was in slow motion and she was powerless to stop it. Dozer let out a low meow and started lapping up the puddle as it dripped off the table onto the rug. Megan scooped him up, deposited him in the bathroom, and shut the door. "For your own good," she said at his loud protests. "Milk, despite popular beliefs, is going to make you sick and give you the runs. It's bad enough I have to clean up this mess without you adding to it."

There was only one sheet left on the paper towel roll. "Of course. Why would anything go right?" She grabbed the roll, a dish towel, and the wet dish cloth. "This kind of sums up my life lately," she said, standing over the mess. "I need to get out of this funk." She knelt in front of the coffee table and sopped up the milk from the table and as much as she could from the rug. "Guess I'm running errands after all. Time to get some carpet cleaner."

She put everything away and let Dozer out of the bathroom. "Don't do any more damage while I'm gone." He let out a long meow. "Okay. I forgive you. It's not like you stopped talking to me. Like someone else who will remain nameless." It didn't matter if Megan said her name or not. Not with the way she seemed to be woven into her heart.

❖

"Happy Thanksgiving," Tara said as the last child left with his mother. She retrieved her phone from her desk. There had been no text from Megan the last ten times she'd checked and there still wasn't. She could try texting her again or maybe even calling. Tara was pretty sure that it was a recording day and Megan would probably be working. She wasn't sure exactly what time she was done.

She slipped her phone in her pocket only to have it vibrate two seconds later. It was her mother calling. What did she want? Tara didn't care to find out. She slipped the phone back into her pocket.

She was tempted to drive to Megan's and sit outside her door until Megan came home but thought better of that idea. A phone call later might be better. She drove to Anna's house and started supper so that it would be ready when Anna and Brandon got home.

Her mother called three more times before leaving a voicemail.

"Hello, Tara. Your father and I will be expecting you and Michael for Thanksgiving dinner, seeing you have celebrated that sacred holiday without us for the last…let's see, um, seven years. Michael's parents are dead, so I know you won't be spending the day with them. So, you have no excuse." Tara had no idea what else she had to say because she turned the voicemail off. Life was enough of a challenge lately without throwing her parents into the mix.

Fuck them and fuck Megan if she couldn't respond to a text. No. Not fuck Megan. Tara didn't answer her texts or calls for three days. She deserved whatever punishment Megan wanted to dish out. She wasn't mad at Megan for ignoring her. She cared so much for her. She was mad at herself for the way she hurt Megan. She needed to figure out a way to make it better. Her heart depended on it.

Chapter Eighteen

Tara put the last of the dishes in the dishwasher and wiped her hands on a dish towel. "I'm going to go out for a while," she said to Anna.

"Don't stay out too late. It's a school night," Anna teased her.

"No, it's not. Thanksgiving vacation. Remember?"

"I know I was just funning you. Mom called me. Tried to guilt me into going there for dinner," Anna said.

"What did you say?"

"That I was busy. She pretended to cry, then got mad when I didn't change my mind."

"Sounds like Mom. I don't know how late I'll be. Don't wait up."

"I never do. Oh, and I fixed the zipper on your coat."

"Thanks. You're the best," Tara said.

"I know."

Tara tapped the steering wheel on her drive to Megan's house. Fear mingled with excitement in her stomach threatening to come up her throat. Megan's car was in the parking lot. So far, so good.

"Please don't hate me," Tara said when Megan opened the door. "I'm sorry."

Megan was silent and Tara couldn't read her face.

"Can I come in?"

Megan stood for several long moments with her arms crossed blocking the doorway. She wasn't making it easy.

"I didn't come here because I need you," Tara started. "I mean, I need you. But not for court."

Tara was sure her heart was going to beat out of her chest. She unzipped her jacket as the sweat started to soak through her shirt. Was it worth all this trouble? There were hundreds, maybe thousands of women that would jump at the chance to date her. Well, maybe not that many, but some for sure. Did she really need this one? The answer was yes. She needed to at least try.

"I really would like to explain." She let out a groan. "Please." She waited several beats. "You're being an ass."

"I'm being an ass?"

"Finally. Something we can agree on."

Megan did her best not to smile. It *was* funny, but she was still hurt. And yes, she did agree. She was being an ass, and at the moment she didn't care.

"I told Jackson to settle with Michael for whatever he could get. I told him I wanted to see you, to talk to you. To kiss you if you'll let me." She paused. "I didn't tell him that last part."

"What?" Megan was confused.

"I repeat, can I come in? Please."

Megan stepped aside. Okay, she thought. But I'm not going to offer her something to drink.

Tara stepped past her and slipped off her coat. "Can I get a glass of water, please?"

Damn it. Megan grabbed a glass from the cupboard and filled it with water from the tap. Okay, she thought. But I'm not offering her any ice. She silently handed the glass to Tara.

"Thank you." Tara took the glass into the living room and sat on the couch.

Megan followed her and sat in the chair across from her.

"I couldn't stand being away from you. I know that's very forward of me to say, but at this point I don't care. I've lived most of my life the way other people wanted me to. I'm done with that. I did what Jackson told me to do. I've never gotten divorced before, so I didn't know what I was supposed to do. But I came to the conclusion that you are more important to me than the money. I don't want to fight Michael. I just want it over with. I want to get on with my own life and very much want you in it."

Tara had given up God knows how much money for the chance to be with her. But the hurt wasn't going to be magically washed away with Tara's words. No matter how wonderful they sounded.

"Can you say something? Anything?"

Megan wasn't sure what to say. So she remained silent.

"Tell me you feel the same. Tell me you hate me. Tell me to go to hell if that's what you're thinking."

That wasn't what she was thinking. "I need time to digest this."

"I guess that's better than telling me to go to hell." She sipped her water. "What can I do to help you with that? I'll answer any questions you have."

Questions. Questions. Did she have any questions? *What are your intentions, sir?* Megan almost laughed at the stupidity of the thought. "I don't think I have any questions right now. But I reserve the right to ask if any come to me."

"Of course. I want to stress that I told Jackson to settle as quickly as he can so we can get this over with, because I want to be with you."

"Yeah. I got that."

The silence that filled the room became uncomfortable. It was so unusual to have that feeling when Tara was so close by. They'd never had even a gap in their conversations. Was the crack between them too wide to leap across?

"I'll give you all the time you need." Tara rose. "You know how to get a hold of me. And, Megan," she said, "I really hope you do. Please think about what I said. I have feelings for you. Real feelings. Even if you don't feel the same, I wanted you to know that." She set her nearly full glass of water on the kitchen counter on her way out the door.

Dozer jumped up on Megan's lap. "Where were you when I needed you? Hiding, you coward." She ran a hand over his back, and he showed his appreciation by raising his rear and putting it in her face, whipping his tail against her cheek. "Thanks for that. Oh, buddy, what am I going to do? I still have so many feelings for her. But damn. Can I trust her?" When he didn't answer, she went on. "I know, go with my gut. My gut gets all in knots when I'm around her—or even when I think of her."

Lately she hadn't wanted to think about her. But now things

had changed. Or had they? That was the big question. "What's the answer?"

Dozer leaped off her lap and headed toward the kitchen. He was gone all of three seconds when he stuck his head back into the living room and let out a loud meow. "You do not need food," Megan said. "And you aren't helping me figure this out. If there's one person I thought could help me, it would be you, even if you are just a cat."

He let out another meow. "I didn't mean *just* a cat. You're a very special cat—that obviously likes his food bowl filled to the brim." Megan realized, as she got up to pour more food into his bowl, that she was stalling. She didn't want to think about what Tara had just confessed to her. She wanted to stay hurt—at least a little while longer. Hurt was a feeling she could trust. She wasn't so sure about her other feelings.

❖

Tara sat in her car for a long time. She'd hoped that Megan would come running after her confessing her feelings and saying she wanted to start again. Or at least say something positive. No such luck. But, yeah, her saying she needed time was better than saying there was no chance at all. At least there was that—a small shred of hope to hold on to.

"You look down," Anna said when Tara joined her on the living room couch. "Something happen?"

Tara gave her the latest news. "So, everything is still up in the air. I hope it's okay with you that I told Jackson to settle. I have no idea what that will mean money-wise."

"How many times do I have to tell you to take care of you and not worry about me?"

"I'm thinking at least a dozen more. Maybe fifteen. But space them out. Don't tell me all at once."

"At least you haven't lost your sense of humor," Anna said.

"But I feel like I've lost so much in the past several weeks."

Anna took her hand. "I know. But this is just the first step. That's always the hardest. It will feel much better when you're back on your feet. You get to pick out your own place to live, decorate it the way you want. Do what you want to do in your spare time. Date who you want to date."

"The person I want to date might tell me she's not interested anymore." That terrified her. Much more than she thought it should.

"There are other women out there. You haven't even had a chance to explore. What's so special about this one?"

"Her dimples, for one thing." Tara smiled. "I know. I know. There are plenty of women out there with dimples. She's kind. She's funny. She's smart."

"Hey, she dated Michael. How smart could she be?" Anna raised her eyebrows to show she was joking.

"I married him. How stupid does that make me?"

"Hey."

"Stop calling myself stupid. Got it. I can list all her good qualities, but there's just something about her. It's like, I don't know, like my soul leaps for joy when I'm around her. Do you know what I mean?"

"I do. That's the way I felt about Nathan."

"I'm sorry. Here I am going on and on about the possibility of losing someone I never really had and you lost Nathan. That's very insensitive of me."

"Stop. A paper cut doesn't hurt any less just because your neighbor cut off his foot with a chain saw."

Tara shook her head. "Um, I'm going to have to think about that one for a while."

"I'm just saying that your pain isn't any less because someone else has suffered too." She stood. "I'm going to get us some wine. I think this conversation calls for some libation. Do you want a snack to go with it? I made some brownies while you were gone."

That made Tara think of the first time she met Megan in person and they shared a brownie. What had she thought of her then? Was the attraction instant? No, she was too focused on leaving Michael and having Megan help her. She did like her from the start, though.

"Earth to Tara. Brownie?"

"No, thanks."

Anna returned with two glasses and a full bottle of wine. She set them on the coffee table. Tara poured wine into each glass as Anna returned to the kitchen for the brownies. "Brought you one anyway. If you don't eat it, I will." She set a small plate in front of Tara.

"You know if you give it to me, I'll eat it."

"I know." Anna settled on the couch next to Tara. She took a sip of her wine. "So, back to your woman." She laughed. "I have to get used to that still. You always seemed so straight." She paused. "And straightlaced."

"First of all, she's not *my* woman. And I was never really straightlaced. I had no interest in sleeping with men and I was too afraid to sleep with women." She took a bite of her brownie. One thing was for sure. Her sister was a great baker.

"That doesn't sound like a good place to be."

"It wasn't. But it was pounded into my head that being a lesbian, or even seeming like I was one, would send me straight to hell."

"You don't believe that, do you?"

"I did at the time. I don't now. I don't believe much of what they told me. Didn't they pound that into your head too?"

"Interestingly enough, no. Maybe because I was boy crazy. I had a million lectures on premarital sex and the wicked ways of men."

"Yet they allowed you to date and didn't push you into marriage, like they did me. Tell me," she said. She sipped her wine before proceeding. "Did you have any idea that I'm gay? Truth."

Anna seemed to think about it for several long beats. She shook her head. "No. I knew you didn't date much, but I thought it was a moral thing, not a gay thing. How long did you know you were gay?"

Tara took a deep breath. "I don't know. I think it happened more in dribs and drabs. I was in denial so long I'm not sure when I finally figured it out." She gave it a few more moments of thought. "I think I've always known I was gay. I just didn't realize it."

Anna choked on the mouthful of wine she'd just sipped. It took a few moments for her to get it under control. "Surprisingly enough, I understand that. What are you going to do about Megan?" Anna asked bringing the conversation full circle.

"I did everything I could for the moment. Now it's in her court. I hope to God she still wants to play ball."

Chapter Nineteen

Megan had done nothing but think about what Tara had told her the day before. She'd come to no conclusions. She needed someone to talk to—throw some ideas around. She went in search of Dozer and found him sleeping on her bed. She lay down next to him and ran a hand over his black coat. He stretched and yawned and seemed to give her his full attention.

"Help me figure this out, buddy. One, I have a lot of feelings for her, and she said she has feelings for me too." She held up one finger. "Two, she hurt me." Another finger went up. "Three, she said she was sorry and gave up on fighting for money so she could be with me." She put her hand down. "You're right, Dozer. That's a big thing. More money could change her life for the better. But then again, being with me could change her life for the better too." She sat up. "'Cause I am worth it. And you know what?" She turned to the cat. "She is too. She's worth the risk. No relationship is guaranteed. There is risk in every single one of them."

Dozer yawned and closed his eyes again.

"Yeah. You sleep on it. Because I think I figured this out. I appreciate your help. Gotta go." She kissed him on the top of his head.

Her sister answered the door with Harper in her arms. "Happy Thanksgiving." She stepped back so Megan could go past her. "Daddy's in the living room."

Megan took Harper from Jill's arms. "Come here, my sweetie. Your momma needs her hands free so she can make us some yummy food." She made her way to the living room and greeted her father sitting with his feet up in the recliner, beer in hand. "Who's winning?" She nodded at the football game on the television.

"Dallas is ahead, but not by much. Sit and watch it with me. I haven't seen you in forever." He lowered the volume on the TV.

Megan sat on the couch and bounced Harper on her knee. "I know. Life sometimes gets in the way of—well—life."

"I get it. I've been busy too. Found me a nice lady to play bingo with."

"You did? That's great. Tell me about her."

When her father finished singing the praises of his new *lady friend,* as he called her, Megan said, "She sounds wonderful."

"What about you? Your sister told me you broke up with Mike. I'm sorry to hear that. I was looking forward to meeting him. Jill said he was married. Guess that would have thrown a wrench in your wedding if you'd made it that far." He laughed at his own joke. "Sorry. Don't mean to make light of it. Must have been hard. How are you doing?"

"I'm okay. It wasn't meant to be."

"That's a good attitude. Got anyone else on the hook? I mean, you're probably fighting them off with a stick."

Megan laughed. "Yes. I fight them off with a stick. That's why I'm still single. People don't like being beaten. Well, some people do, but I'm not into that."

"Into what?" Jill entered the room.

"She's been beating people," their father said.

"I've heard that about her. What do you want to drink?" Jill asked her. She set a plate of cheese puffs on the table between them.

"A beer would be great. And bring one for Harper too. She seems like a Budweiser kind of gal."

Jill put her arms out to Harper and the little girl reached for her. "She's more of a baby formula kind of gal, and it's time for her nap." She picked her up. "Wave bye-bye."

Megan waved. "Bye-bye."

And Harper waved back. "Ooh. That's so cute. See ya later, baby girl."

As Jill walked back through the living room, Megan asked, "Anything I can help with?"

"Nope. Todd has it under control."

"Oh, good. He's a much better cook than I am anyway."

Jill disappeared through the swinging door into the kitchen and reappeared with a bottle of beer that she handed to Megan.

Dinner as always was delicious, and the company was great. The conversation was light but lively. Their dad said his goodbyes and was off to have dessert with his new love interest. Todd was off with Harper in the playroom, giving Jill and Megan a chance to talk.

"You seem like you're in a really good mood," Jill said as she settled on the couch next to Megan.

"I am. Tara came by and said she told her lawyer to settle for whatever he can get for her. She wants it over and wants back into my life."

"And you're going to let her?" Jill said.

"You say that like it would be a bad thing. You're the one that said she didn't have a choice when she stopped talking to me. She did have a choice, and she chose me."

"I know I said that. But I've been thinking about it. Are you sure you're not just a rebound? I don't want her to hurt you. Again."

"I thought you would be more supportive than this." Megan went into the kitchen for another bottle of beer. She grabbed one for Jill as well. She was going to need one for this conversation.

"Thanks," Jill said. "It's not that I'm not supportive. I support you and any decision you make. I'm just worried about you."

"You don't need to be." She tilted the bottle of beer up too high as she took a swig, and a stream of beer trickled down her chin. She wiped it with the back of her hand.

"You don't know how to drink from a bottle, of course I worry about you."

Megan attempted to give her a dirty look. She wasn't sure if she pulled it off. "I know how to drink, thank you very much."

"Just think about it. That's all I ask."

"All I've been doing is thinking about it. I told Tara I needed time to think. I haven't given her any kind of response yet."

"When did all this happen?"

"Yesterday. Why?"

"Don't rush into this."

Megan shook her head. She didn't rush into this. She let it bounce around in her head since Tara told her. She'd hardly thought about anything else. And now Jill was putting doubts in her mind.

"I'm planning to take it slow. I'll keep my eyes open for any red flags."

"'Cause you're the master of red flags."

The heat rose up Megan's neck. "What does that mean?"

"Don't shoot the messenger. I'm just stating facts. You didn't see the red flags when Aliza was cheating on you. You didn't know Mike was married. You haven't been the best at spotting these things."

"They both lied to me. Tara hasn't. You can't put her in the same box as them."

Jill put her hands up. "Okay. I'll trust your judgment. But you can't stop me from worrying."

Damn it. Was there any truth to what Jill was saying? Was she just a rebound or even an experiment for Tara?

"Now I've fucked up your mood. I'm sorry."

"Language," Todd said, coming back into the room with Harper in tow. "I was just wondering if you wanted to get Harper ready for bed, or if you wanted me to." Jill had lucked out when she met him. He turned out to be a great husband and father.

"Jill's gonna do it and I'm gonna help," Megan declared. "Gimme that kid." She rose and took Harper from Todd.

"I'll get her bottle ready," he said.

"Jill, up with you. Let's get this little pumpkin ready for night-night." She started down the hall to the nursery. "Come on, sweetie," she whispered to Harper. "We can figure this out without Momma."

"Momma is right behind you. Don't be telling that kid bad things about me."

"Never," Megan said.

Megan got Harper changed with the diaper and night clothes Jill handed her. She gave her a kiss on the top of her head and handed her to Jill. "I don't want to be blamed for making her go to bed," she said. She gave Jill a squeeze from behind. "I'm going to head home. Thanks for a great day."

"Don't forget the doggy bag Todd made for you. It's in the kitchen."

"Yep." She said good-bye to him as she passed him in the hallway on his way to the nursery with a bottle for Harper. Yeah, Jill found a good one for sure. She'd thought maybe she'd found her *good one* in Tara. Now she wasn't so sure. Maybe a conversation was in order before she made up her mind.

Her mood was in the toilet by the time she pulled into her parking lot. How could she have dropped so low from the high she was riding only that afternoon? The possibility that she would be a rebound for Tara was the answer. She had the answer. Now she needed the questions.

❖

Can we talk? Megan typed on her phone. She hit send and the text went invisibly through the air to Tara's phone the next morning. She'd hardly slept at all. Was all this worth it? It would be if Tara was being truthful. Megan was convinced she wasn't lying to her. But the question was, was she lying to herself?

She didn't have to wait long for a response. *Absolutely. When and where*

The place we first met. Noon today?

I'll be there.

Tara was already there, seated at the same table when Megan arrived. She had a cup of what Megan assumed was a cappuccino. A bottle of water was in front of the empty seat with a brownie on a plate and two forks in the middle of the table. Megan couldn't help but smile.

Tara rose when she saw Megan and stepped forward with her arms out. Megan hesitated only a moment before stepping into them for a very long hug.

"Sorry," Tara said. "I hope that was okay to do."

"You didn't see me fighting you off, did you?"

They sat and Tara gave Megan a smile. "I hope that's a good sign."

Megan didn't want to give her false hope if in the end she

decided that being with Tara would only cause more heartbreak. "How have you been?" Megan thought she was prepared with her questions. She wasn't sure why she was hesitating now. Maybe it was the way she felt in Tara's arms only moments before. Home. Tara felt like home.

"I'm okay. This break from school is nice. I've missed you." She reached for Megan's hand but pulled back before taking it. "You?"

"Missed you too. But there is something I need to know."

"You can ask me anything."

Megan took a deep breath. Why was this so hard? Because she didn't want to know the answer if it would keep her from being with Tara. And she so desperately wanted to be with her.

"Megan?"

"Um. Yeah. How can I be sure this isn't just a rebound situation for you? I mean, you just left your husband, and you know I like women. Maybe I'm just the most convenient available female." There. She said it. She held her breath waiting for Tara's answer. She didn't have to wait long.

"If I was looking for a rebound relationship, I certainly wouldn't have chosen you."

What? "What? Gee, thanks."

"I mean I wouldn't have chosen the person Michael was involved with. Not you as a person. I've never felt this way about anyone before. Yes, I've had crushes. Plenty of them, and I might have acted on them if they had been reciprocated—not while I was married, of course."

Megan nodded. So far so good. "Go on."

"While I cared for Michael, and I did, I never really loved him. How could I? I wasn't looking to rush into another relationship. But meeting you, spending time with you, changed that."

"Are you sure you aren't fooling yourself?"

"Fooling myself? How? About my feelings for you?"

"That's part of it, yes."

"I am as sure as a person can be. When we kissed, I felt so connected to you. My feelings are real. You are everything I dreamed of finding in a person."

"You know I'm not perfect, right? I mean, I'm damn close."

Tara laughed. "Your humor is the first thing that drew me to you. I know you aren't perfect. I mean, I know you can hold a grudge." She smiled. "I'm not perfect either, as I have already demonstrated by my stupid decisions."

"I'm not going to argue that point. See how agreeable I can be?"

"You are definitely agreeable when you aren't hating me." Tara sipped her coffee but kept her eyes on Megan.

"I never hated you. I never could. I was hurt."

"I know. And I'm so sorry. So sorry. You said my feelings for you was part of it. What's the other part?"

"You've never been with a woman before."

"Yes. Is that a problem? I'm a quick learner. I'll read books, watch videos, take notes. We can practice a lot until I get everything right." The smile that lit up Tara's face was hard to resist.

Megan smiled in return. "That's not what I mean. How do you know it's what's right for you?"

"Oh, believe me, it is. Being with Michael was okay. I didn't want to vomit or anything. But kissing you was on a whole other level. I've never wanted Michael the way I want you."

"You still want me?" Megan already knew the answer. For some reason she needed to hear Tara say it.

"I can show you right now if you want?"

"In the middle of this café? You aren't even out." Megan sipped her water. The thought of kissing Tara again made her mouth go dry and sent a tingle to her center.

"What a great way to come out."

"Let's talk about that." There was still more Megan needed to know. "You would be willing to come out? Publicly? To your family? What about work?"

Tara was more than willing to answer anything Megan asked her if it meant they had a chance together. "That's a whole lot of questions. Yes. Publicly. I've already told my sister. I don't care one way or the other if my parents know. My relationship with them, as you know, sucks. To put it bluntly, I don't plan on having them in my life. I've already cut them off for the most part." She paused while she thought about work. Living in western New York State offered protection for her job. She wasn't sure how some of the parents would feel if they knew she was gay. Did it really matter? "As far as my job goes, I wouldn't deny it if asked, but I probably wouldn't shout it from the rooftops either."

"I can live with that."

"Are you out to everyone you know?" Tara said as gently as she could. She didn't want Megan to think she was being snarky.

"I am. I don't lead with that when I meet someone. But I don't have any problem with anyone knowing. I do get some shit from people that say I can't make up my mind liking both men and women."

"My turn for an important question. Do you think you would miss being with men? I'm a very monogamous person. I wouldn't want an open relationship."

"This might sound terrible, but I much prefer women. Yes, I've been with men, but there always seems to be something lacking. I love women's hearts so much more. So, no, I wouldn't miss being with men. And I'm monogamous too."

Tara sipped her coffee in an attempt to hide the huge smile that seemed to be spreading across her face. Megan hadn't said they could be together. Yet. But her response was definitely heading in that direction.

"Where do we go from here?" Megan asked.

"If you're saying yes let's go for it, then I would suggest we go back to your place." Tara had never been so bold. She hoped Megan was getting what she was hinting at.

"Then I guess I'm saying yes. But I have one more important question."

Just when Tara thought they'd worked everything out, Megan seemed to have more reservations. Tara hoped her answer wouldn't change anything. "What is it?"

"Can we eat this brownie before we go?"

Chapter Twenty

Tara grabbed Megan by the collar as soon as Megan closed her apartment door behind them. She couldn't wait a minute longer to kiss her again. Her breath caught in her throat a moment before their lips met. She was wet in an instant.

She wasn't sure if the moans that permeated the air came from her or Megan. Turned out it was both. Everything became a blur as their hands moved over each other and their lips crashed together. Tara pushed her tongue between Megan's lips and their tongues joined in the dance of desire.

When Tara put her hand under Megan's shirt and took possession of Megan's breast, the kiss ended as quickly as it had started, Megan pulled back. "Wait. Wait," she said breathlessly.

The beating in Tara's chest intensified. Fear crept through her. Had Megan changed her mind? "What?" She could hardly get the word to come out of her mouth. A mouth that had been so entangled with Megan's that she'd lost all sense of being.

"Are you sure you want to do this?"

Tara still clung tightly to Megan, afraid to let go. "Yes. Don't you?"

"Oh my God, yes. But you said you don't want to do anything while you're still married. I don't want to do anything you aren't ready for."

"The divorce papers are filed. In my heart it's over. I want you.

I want all of you. Now." It was more of a demand than a statement. She slipped a hand down Megan's pants and felt how wet she was. "It feels like you want it too." Her lips crashed into Megan's before Megan had a chance to respond. But the groan and her body's reaction to Tara's touch was answer enough.

Tara walked Megan back toward the kitchen table and bent her over it. She continued kissing her, not only with her mouth, but it felt like her whole body was involved.

Megan wrestled her way out from under her and stood up. "No. Not like this. I want this to be special for you. You deserve romance. You deserve to be made love to, not sex on the kitchen table." Her voice trembled. "Stay here. I'll be right back." She softly kissed Tara on the lips. "Don't go anywhere." She disappeared down the hall.

Tara pulled out a chair and sat. It took a minute or two to catch her breath. It was shocking to her how her body reacted to kissing and touching Megan. Yes, her feelings were real. There was no doubt in her mind.

It seemed to take forever for Megan to return, but it was probably only a few minutes. Megan reappeared and held out her hand. Tara took it and allowed herself to be led to the bedroom. The lights were off, but several candles illuminated the room. The bedspread and blankets were pulled back. "You're sure?" Megan asked.

"I have never been so sure of anything in my life."

"Then come here." Megan pulled her close enough to kiss, but not so close that she couldn't unbutton Tara's blouse. She pulled the shirt from Tara's shoulders and let it slip to the floor. She made short work of Tara's bra, which joined the shirt on the floor. Megan stepped back to admire her. "You are so beautiful."

How could Megan's eyes sweeping up and down across her body make her feel so alive? So wanted.

"Your turn," Tara said. Megan's shirt and bra were soon discarded in the pile. Just the sight of Megan's body was a turn-on. Each step, each new experience was a revelation, and Tara's body reacted. She pulled Megan into an embrace and kissed her lips, making her way down her neck to her breasts. She sucked on a nipple and let her tongue roll around it, savoring the salty taste and the feeling of it in her mouth. How could something so simple be so complex and all consuming?

The rest of their clothes were quickly discarded, and they were totally skin to skin, body to body. Soul to soul.

Megan led Tara to the bed and gently pushed her down. Kneeling in front of her, she gently parted Tara's legs and kissed her inner thighs, moving agonizingly slowly toward Tara's center. She reached Tara's most sacred space and, without warning, plunged her tongue into her.

Tara closed her eyes against the unbelievable feeling. Lights seemed to be exploding behind her eyelids. She thought she moaned out loud but wasn't sure. Her attention was hyperfocused on Megan and the delicious things she was doing to her body. To her very being. Yes. This was the way it was supposed to be. She attempted to put her hands on the back of Megan's head—not that she needed any encouragement—but her arms wouldn't move. She was limp with the sensations coursing through her.

Megan's hands were on her breasts and Tara's nipples stood at attention against them. She wasn't sure how much more she could take before she would explode completely and disappear into space. She didn't have long to wait. She felt the orgasm from her toes to the top of her head. Her whole body was throbbing.

The tears that streamed from her eyes surprised her as Megan moved up next to her. She gently wiped the tears from her face. "I don't know why I'm crying," Tara said when she was able to form a sentence.

"Are you alright?"

"Yes. I'm just…" She paused as she tried to find the right words. "That was unbelievable. My emotions…I mean. Yes. I'm just so happy to be here with you."

Megan kissed her on the lips. "Me too. You're shivering. Climb all the way onto the bed and I can cover you up."

"I want to—"

"Shh," Megan said. "We've got time."

With a bit of difficulty, Tara moved onto the bed, her body not totally recovered. Megan climbed up next to her and pulled the covers over both of them before she wrapped her naked body against her.

"I want to touch you," Tara said. "I need to." She didn't wait for an answer and ran her fingers over Megan's nipples. The moan that escaped from Megan's lips urged her on. She'd never touched another woman before, and the softness of Megan's skin was incredible. The covers were pulled back far enough to expose Megan's body. Tara was in awe at the wonder of it.

Megan placed a hand on each side of Tara's face, pulled her in, and kissed her. Deeply.

How could her body react so strongly so soon after such a powerful orgasm? Tara was astounded. Every kiss, every touch affected her. It was more than just being with a woman. It was being with Megan.

Tara pulled back and looked at the woman next to her. The room was dim, lit only by the light of the full moon streaming through the window and the candles Megan had placed about. Megan's features were softly illuminated, making her look almost ethereal. Was she real? Was this real? How was it even possible? The beat of Tara's heart gave her the answer as she stroked Megan's cheek and took in her scent.

"Okay?" Megan asked.

Tara nodded, afraid if she tried to speak, she would choke with all the intoxicating emotions rushing through her. Every moment they'd shared, every laugh, the betrayal they'd both shared, had led to this moment, and Tara was so grateful.

She leaned into Megan and kissed her. Megan's soft lips yielded, letting Tara deepen the kiss. Tara melted into her and the world dissolved. Nothing existed except the two of them. The mix of desire and vulnerability was something Tara had never allowed herself to explore before. Not fully. Not like this.

Tara trailed her fingers down Megan's stomach and realized she was trembling. Not from fear—it was something else, something new and overwhelming. She felt like she'd been waiting for this moment her whole life. She moved her hand lower and slid one finger between Megan's folds. She was surprised how wet Megan was. Megan moaned and spread her legs farther apart, spurring Tara on. Tara's own body responded as she felt Megan's excitement heighten. She moved first one finger, then a second and a third inside

Megan. The rhythm of her movements seemed to match the rhythm of her own beating heart.

Keeping the movement of her fingers, Tara broke the kiss, leaned down, and took Megan's nipple in her mouth, rolling her tongue around it before sucking it in, tasting the goodness. She moved from one to the other giving each one equal attention.

Megan's body stiffened and a low throaty groan emanated from her. Tara felt her tighten and throb around her fingers. She couldn't help but smile. Megan sucked in a deep breath as Tara extracted her fingers. She kissed her way up to Megan's cheek.

"Wow," Megan said breathlessly. "I can't believe you've never done that before."

"I got a *wow* on my first time?"

"Let me add amazing."

Placing small kisses on Megan's shoulders, Tara snuggled in close. Megan wrapped an arm around her shoulder. "How are you doing?"

"I don't believe I've ever felt this content in my whole life."

"Content is good."

"Let me add happy." She looked into Megan's eyes. "How about you?"

"Ditto. Content and happy and so grateful you're here with me."

"There isn't any other place I'd rather be."

Megan ran a single finger down the center of Tara's chest. The touch was featherlight, but it sent a ripple of heat through her. "What are the rules about doing this again?" Tara whispered.

"It's mandatory."

"Like right now?"

"Like right now." Megan rolled over on top of Tara, slipping a leg between her thighs, creating just the right amount of pressure in just the right spot. Megan moved gently but with determination against her, making Tara's heart ache in the best way. She smiled as round two got underway.

❖

"Breakfast?" Megan asked. "Or do you want to sleep in? As I recall you didn't get much sleep last night."

Tara cuddled closer to Megan, kissing her neck. "Who needs sleep when I've got you so close?"

"So, breakfast can wait?"

Tara sat up. "No. I'm starving. I've worked up quite an appetite, thanks to you."

"You're welcome. What are you going to make us?" Megan pulled the covers up higher.

Tara pulled the blankets down to Megan's waist. "I'm going to make *you*. I need more practice with this gay stuff." She took possession of one of Megan's breasts and felt her nipple harden against her palm.

"I think you've got this gay stuff down pat. But a little more practice wouldn't hurt." Megan pulled Tara down and kissed her.

Tara's phone rang from somewhere in the room. "Ignore that."

"What if it's important?" Megan asked.

"There is nothing more important than you in this moment." Tara resumed their kiss.

It was another hour before they hauled themselves out of bed and decided to go out to breakfast—or was it lunch that late in the day?

Tara listened to the voicemail from earlier as they waited for their food to arrive. It was from Jackson. "Please give me a call so we can set up a meeting. I've got some news for you."

"I don't know if I should be happy or nervous," she said to Megan. "But I'm definitely leaning toward nervous."

Chapter Twenty-One

"A re you sure you don't want me to go with you?" Megan asked Tara. Jackson had given no indication of what the news was, and Tara didn't ask.

"I appreciate that. I really do. But I need to act like a big girl and finish this on my own. I'll give you a call later and fill you in." She gave Megan a kiss on the lips, marveling at how natural it felt. They'd spent the whole weekend together, but Tara thought it would be best to spend Sunday night at home—well, at her sister's home. It was hard to say good-bye, even for a little while.

Tara's meeting was after work on Monday. She wasn't looking forward to the day at all. The kids were always extra wound up after vacation. She would be glad to find out how the negotiations were going but dreaded the possibility of bad news. But whatever happened, she could deal with it as long as she had Megan.

"Text me when you get home," Megan said. "I'm so glad we got to spend this time together."

"You make it sound like it's all over with," Tara said.

Megan pulled her in close and wrapped the scarf that hung from Tara's shoulders around her neck. "This is just the beginning." She kissed her—gently at first—and then harder as their passion grew.

Tara had trouble catching her breath when she finally pulled away. "If I don't leave now, I might never leave."

Megan smiled. Dimples. "That's alright by me. I'll clean out half the closet and dresser for you." She wiggled her eyebrows.

"That's a little fast. Even for me."

"I'm just kidding. But I'm willing to clean out one drawer. Give you," Megan scrunched up half her face, "three, no, four hangers in the closet and even your own toothbrush."

"I thought the toothbrush you gave me this morning was going to be my own toothbrush. Don't tell me it was used."

"Only by Dozer and only a couple dozen times." Another smile. More dimples.

If Tara didn't leave right now, she knew she would be tempted to stay another night, and that meant very little sleep. She knew she wouldn't be able to function at work that way. She reluctantly extracted herself from Megan's arms and backed away. "Tell Dozer to keep his fangs off my toothbrush from now on." She gave Megan a quick kiss on the nose, turned, and headed toward the door. "Text ya soon." She waved a hand in the air, not daring to turn around and look at Megan again. She quietly closed the door behind her and leaned against it. She let out a sigh of contentment mixed with a longing to return to the arms of the woman she'd just left. She'd waited all her life for someone. Now she knew who that someone was. She was determined to make this work.

❖

Was that a sigh Megan heard through the closed door? She was tempted to open it and pull Tara back into her arms. Who would have thought that the late night phone call that had left her shaking would turn into this—a woman who made her tremble in a whole different way. A marvelous, oh so delicious way. The weekend had been more than she could have hoped for.

They were moving fast, but she didn't care. It was right. They were right. She would just explain it that way to her sister when she told her. "We both know what she's going to say. Don't we?" she said to Dozer, who had joined her in the kitchen and was eyeing his nearly full bowl of food. "She'll say, *I thought you were going to take it slow.*" Megan raised the pitch of her voice a level or two even though her sister didn't sound that way. "Well, you know what? I don't care. And I don't care if you think there isn't enough food in your bowl, because there is."

Dozer let out a pitiful meow in response.

"Okay, bossy. Just a little more." Megan poured several pieces of dry cat food from the container on the counter into his bowl. He leaped on it, apparently satisfied that he'd gotten his way.

"And leave Tara's toothbrush alone." There. She'd told him. She looked around the apartment, which now seemed so empty without Tara. How could that be? How could she leave such a void when she'd only spent the weekend there? Friday evening till Sunday evening wasn't that long. Megan had lived here for the past four years, and it never seemed lonely—until now.

It was only a little after eight, but Megan got herself ready for bed. She climbed in and reached for the pillow that Tara had used the last few nights. She brought it to her face and breathed in Tara's scent. She was going to be in trouble if this didn't work out. She was already so head over heels. She'd never fallen this fast for anyone. She hoped Tara felt the same way about her. She seemed to. Megan was sure she did.

She got out of bed, restless, and wandered into the living room, bringing the pillow with her. Maybe doing research for one of their future podcasts would help get her mind off Tara. She sat on the couch, retrieved her laptop from the coffee table, and fired it up. She opened the document with the list of ideas for shows and started at the top.

"Okay. What do I want to learn about women who made a difference in history?" She tapped her chin. "Let's see what the old Google has to say." She typed in the phrase and came up with a list. "Hmm. Theodora, Empress of Byzantium." There wasn't much information on her. "Let's start with someone a little more modern." Her thoughts returned to Tara. She'd certainly changed Megan's recent history. "Keep your mind on work," she reminded herself. She skipped down the list, the first African American woman to hold a pilot's license, first woman to reach the top of Mount Everest. She stopped at Marie Curie, who won two Nobel Prizes and made groundbreaking discoveries about radioactivity. "Let's start with her. Tara was certainly radioactive." Shit. This wasn't working.

Her phone pinged from the bedroom with a text. She closed her laptop, set it back on the coffee table, and hurried to the bedroom. Her heart did a little dance in her chest.

I'm home. Had a truly wonderful time with you. Can't wait to see you again. Followed by a little pink heart.

Don't make too much of that, she told herself. But she couldn't help it. She screenshot the text so it didn't get lost amongst the thousands, probably millions of texts they were sure to send each other over the next years. Years. Yes, Megan was thinking ahead to a lifetime with Tara. It might have been a dangerous thought, but it was a risk she was willing to take. Tara was worth it. She replied with a simple word, *Ditto*, and a purple heart of her own.

Tara's day went much better than she had anticipated, but she had to keep pulling her mind back to the task at hand. It kept drifting in the direction of Megan—and occasionally to her meeting with Jackson.

Thankfully, it was somewhat warmer when she walked to her car after class ended. The traffic was surprisingly light on the drive. Maybe the day would hold more surprises, and Jackson would have good news for her.

He was in with another client when she arrived, so she took the opportunity to text Megan. *Hope your day is going well. I'm waiting for Jackson. Just wanted you to know I'm thinking 'boutcha.*

Megan's response came just as Jackson showed his client out and greeted Tara. Damn. Tara slipped her phone in her pocket without reading Megan's text.

"Come on in, Tara." Jackson settled down in his big leather chair and leaned back. "Have a seat and we can get started." He pulled a folder from his desk drawer, opened it, and pulled out a sheet of paper. "I've got the figures here. As requested, I got the best settlement I could for you." He slid the paper across the desk to her. "It's not final until you agree and sign it. We can still go to court if you aren't happy with it."

Tara searched his face for clues as to what the paper held before picking it up and reading it. It wasn't the million dollars she had once hoped for. She'd given up on that. But she was surprised at what Jackson had gotten them to agree to.

"As you see there, Michael has to sell the house and give you half of the proceeds. It's estimated to be worth about four hundred thousand dollars after commissions and legal fees and such."

If that was in the paperwork, Tara hadn't come to it yet. She was barely halfway down the page. Tears filled her eyes and spilled over. Jackson was nothing but a blur when she looked up at him. She swiped at her eyes with the heel of her hand, positive she'd just smudged her mascara. "I don't understand. Michael owned the house before we were married."

"Your name is on the deed, which was part of your marriage agreement."

"It was? I mean, I knew he added my name. But didn't know he had to." Tara wondered if that was something her parents did without her knowing. They had insisted on handling all the legal arrangements. She never thought she would be grateful for that.

Jackson pushed a box of tissues across the desk. "I seem to have jumped ahead. Sorry. I'll give you time to finish reading. Check out the back too. There is a list of the items you said you wanted. The underlined ones are what Michael agreed you could have." There weren't many things, other than her personal items that Tara had asked for. It looked like she'd gotten almost all of it. Michael got to keep the fancy coffee maker that he had given her for their fifth anniversary, the large screen TV, and about six other things. She wasn't that attached to any of it. She'd put more on the list than she really wanted in hopes of at least getting some of it.

The tissue Tara used to wipe her eyes was stained with her makeup. Several blinks later and her eyes were clear enough to continue reading. Besides the money from the house, she would get two hundred thousand dollars up front and three thousand dollars a month for two years. After a quick calculation in her head, she realized the total was well over four hundred thousand dollars. Much more than she expected when she decided that Megan was more important than money. "How did you do this?" she asked.

Jackson laughed. "They knew that if we went to court, it would cost them more. I never took that threat off the table. I *might* have also hinted that we *might* have had another woman besides Megan ready to testify to an affair."

"But we didn't have anyone else."

"I know, but they didn't. And I'm sorry, but there must have been more than Megan, or the threat would have been empty." He put his hands up. "It wasn't actually a threat. It was a suggestion."

"A lawyer's suggestion can sound like a threat." Tara laughed. "I don't care how you did it. I'm just glad you did."

Jackson pulled more paperwork out of the folder. "You can keep that breakdown of the figures." He indicated the paper in her hand. "But…" He slid the stack of paper to her and placed a pen on top. "Take your time going through this. It's all the legal mumbo jumbo, but all the figures are exactly what's on the paper you just read. You need to initial each page and then sign and date the last page."

It took only a few minutes to scan each page, initial, and sign. She didn't read every word but trusted Jackson.

"You have a week to get any of your personal items and everything on that list out of the house. The day and time needs to be worked out in advance and Michael won't be there, but he insisted that someone representing him is. His suggestion was"— Jackson thumbed through a notepad—"his friend Pete." He looked up at Tara. "Do you want to agree to that?"

Pete had always been nice to her, and she had gotten together with his wife for coffee a few times. That would work. She nodded.

"Okay. Do you have a day and time you would like to go to the house?"

"Can I take someone with me to help?"

"I would imagine you'll need to. Some of this stuff is heavy, I'm sure. You'll probably need to rent a van or borrow a truck or something."

Tara ran through a list of possible people she could ask for help. Cori's husband was the obvious choice, and he owned a truck. A quick text and she had an answer for Jackson. "Saturday at noon."

"I'll let Michael's lawyer know and get back to you to confirm."

They wrapped up the meeting and Tara headed out to her car. She glanced at the restaurant across the street where she and Megan had dinner after her first meeting with Jackson. Was that when she started falling for her? Probably. All she knew for sure was how she felt about her now. She was on the verge of falling in love. And it felt better than she ever could have imagined.

The text Megan had sent her could wait until she was back in her car out of the winter wind. It whipped around her face, making her ears hurt. Her face was numb by the time she climbed into the driver's seat. Once the sun went down, which it did way too early in late November, the weather could be brutal. She wished she'd parked closer, but the only spot she could find was almost a block away.

Wearing gloves would have been a good idea, had she thought to pick them up from the front seat when she'd gotten out of the car. She doubted they would warm her very cold hands now. One of the first things she was going to buy with the money from her settlement was a remote car starter—not that she could have started her car from a block away. How come she'd never thought about that before? Guess she'd been content to get into a freezing cold car in the winter, it matched her marriage—at least the last couple of years.

Enough of that kind of thinking. Tara fished around her coat pocket for her phone, which she could barely feel with numb fingers.

She pulled up Megan's text. *I've had a very productive day. Did research for the next three podcasts. OK, I tried to do that but couldn't get you out of my head. I know. I know. It's warm and cozy in there and you didn't want to leave. I don't blame you. Let me know how it goes. Better yet, come over and tell me in person.*

Yes. Megan was definitely upward. The text made Tara smile. Stopping over was out of the question. Tara knew that she wouldn't want to leave once she laid eyes—and hands—on Megan, and she'd promised Anna that she would make dinner. The car started on the first try. It hadn't given her any trouble since that day at school. She called Megan through her car.

"Hey, baby," Megan answered. Baby? That was the first time either of them used a pet name and it went straight to Tara's heart.

"Hi. I miss you. It's been a whole night and day without you." She knew it was mushy, but she didn't care. It's what she felt. She was done hiding her feelings.

"I feel the same. How did it go with Jackson?"

Tara gave her the rundown.

"And? Your thoughts? Are you satisfied?"

"It's more than I thought I could get, so absolutely. Jackson certainly earned his very high fee."

"Come over. We can celebrate. I have a bottle of champagne here somewhere. I bought it when we hit a hundred thousand subscribers for the podcast."

Tara pulled out onto the street, thankful that the car that had been parked in front of her was gone. "Why didn't you drink it?"

"I didn't have anyone to share it with. Dozer doesn't like the bubbles, and I don't like to drink alone. That's a lie. I am willing to drink alone. Just not champagne."

"What about the woman you do the podcast with?" Tara forgot her name.

"She celebrated with her husband, and our producer was out of town and I forgot about it by the time she was back. Soooo..." Megan drew the word out. "I'll see you soon?"

"I wish I could. Not tonight. But soon."

"I'm gonna hold you to that."

"I'm gonna hold *you*." More mushy stuff. "Soon. I can't wait."

"Me too."

"As much as I want to keep talking to you, I need to concentrate on driving. It's starting to snow."

"Yes. Go. I want you to stay safe. Think about coming over tomorrow after work. I should be home by four."

"It's a date. I'll bring dinner. See you then." Megan seemed to want to see her as much as she wanted to see Megan. That made Tara very happy and a little scared.

Chapter Twenty-Two

W hy scared?" Anna asked Tara as they loaded the dishwasher together.

Tara couldn't help but tell Anna everything that had transpired between Megan and her—leaving out the intimate details, of course.

"What if it doesn't work out?" Tara asked. "I'm not sure my heart could take that."

Anna filled the soap dispenser, closed the dishwasher, and set it to start at midnight. "First of all, you would survive. You've got a hundred percent survival rate so far. Just look how much you've overcome already. And second, why would you think it wouldn't work out? You said Megan feels the same way you do."

Tara shook her head. She plopped down in a chair. "I don't know. I just want this so bad. You know? I'm not sure I've ever wanted anything so much."

"You're driving yourself crazy when you should be celebrating the good feelings. I think you've found someone really special."

"You're right."

"I usually am." Anna moved a pot from the stove to the sink and filled it with hot water, giving it a squirt of dish soap. "I would like to meet her. Why don't you invite her over for dinner? That way I can ask her what her intentions are toward you."

Tara laughed. "You wouldn't dare."

"I wouldn't. But I'm serious about meeting her."

Anna was right. Megan had been nothing but great since the

very first phone call. She pushed the worry aside. She truly believed they had a bright future ahead of them. She was going to cherish every moment of it. "I was planning on going to her apartment tomorrow. I'll see if she wants to come here instead." Would that mean they wouldn't be spending the night together as Tara had planned? She didn't want to assume that Megan would be welcome to spend the night at Anna's. And she didn't want to have wild and crazy sex with her sister and nephew in the next rooms. She smiled at the thought of having wild and crazy sex with Megan. So far it had been gentle, but very passionate. She wasn't even sure what wild and crazy would entail.

"What the hell are you thinking?" Anna asked.

It brought Tara out of her head—and libido. "What?"

"You had the most wicked smile on your face. No. Never mind. I don't want to know."

"Yeah. You don't want to know."

"Oh. I almost forgot. Is there any chance you can hang with Brandon on Friday night?" She had what Tara would describe as a wicked smile herself. "I. Have. A. Date."

Surprised was an understatement. Anna had never mentioned dating since her husband died. "Of course."

"I won't be out late, so you would still have plenty of time to go to Megan's if you want."

"Who are you going out with?"

"Milton from work. His wife died a year before Nathan did. We have a lot in common. He said he wasn't ready to date until now. I guess I wasn't either."

"Oh, I'm so happy for you." She only wanted the best for her sister. She'd been alone too long, and maybe this Milton person— what kind of a name was Milton—would be just what she needed.

"Slow down there." Anna put her hand out. "It's just a date. We haven't planned our wedding yet."

"I know. Can I be your maid of honor when you do? And help you decide on the flavor for your cake?"

Anna laughed. "You can plan the whole damn thing. Just let me get through Friday evening first."

"Deal." Tara stood. "I'm going to go call Megan about dinner tomorrow and ask her to be my plus-one for your wedding. Oh, I hope…"

"Alright. Enough already. Go call your girlfriend."

Girlfriend. Tara liked the word. Liked the way it sounded when Anna said it. Liked the way it felt in her heart. In the bedroom, Tara sat on the bed, leaned against the headboard, and called Megan.

"Hey there. I was just thinking about you."

"That is quite the coincidence, 'cause I was thinking about you, too. Would you mind if we changed our plans for tomorrow?"

"I will probably cry a lot, yes. Something come up?"

"No need to cry. I was just wondering if you would like to come here for dinner. You can meet my sister and nephew." *Please say yes.*

"Meeting your family? Wow. That's a big step."

"If you're not ready—"

"I would love to. I'm so ready. What time? What's the address? What should I bring? Is it casual or dressy? Do you think your sister will like me? How about wine? I can bring wine."

Tara laughed. "Are you sure you don't have any other questions?"

"I'm thinking."

"Let's see." Tara tried to remember everything Megan had asked. "Come over after work. I'll text you the address. Just bring your beautiful self and wear whatever you want. Or come naked. I would like that. Anna might not, but she would love you otherwise. Did that cover it all?"

"Wine?"

"Just you. Naked or not."

"Not."

"Damn. Maybe I can come to your house for dessert, and we can discuss the possibility of you being naked then." Just the thought sent a jolt through Tara that left her wanting.

"I'm thinking that is an excellent idea."

They finished their phone call and Tara went in search of Anna. Brandon was playing a video game on the TV, while Anna read a book in the corner chair, wrapped in a fuzzy blanket. She looked up when Tara came into the room. "Well?"

"She would be happy to attend your wedding with me." Tara crossed in front of Brandon as fast as she could, trying not to block his view. She sat on the other end of the couch.

"Jerk. What did she say about tomorrow?"

"Oh. She'll be here."

"Great."

"I want to fill you in on my meeting with Jackson." Tara leaned her head toward Brandon and raised her eyebrows, hoping Anna got the message.

She did. "Why don't we go in my room," Anna said.

Brandon twisted his head to see around them as they passed. Tara closed the bedroom door and filled Anna in on what she expected to get from Michael.

"I want you to use that money for you," Anna said. She put up a hand when Tara started to protest. "Brandon can go to public school next year. I've already talked to the principal and counselor there. It's all set. So, there is no argument."

Tara wasn't sure if she should be relieved or annoyed. She settled on relieved. "Are you sure? I want to help—"

"Stop. Really. Buy yourself a nice house. Not that I want you out of here. I kind of like having you around."

"Kind of?"

"Yeah. Just kind of. Buy a new car. A boat. A horse. Go to Peru. I don't care. Just use the money for *you*."

"A horse?"

"Doesn't every kid want a pony? Now is your chance. I truly appreciate everything you have done for me and the kiddo. But it's your time to fly. But not on the pony. That would be dangerous." Anna stood. "Thank you for updating me. This discussion is over. Now if you don't mind, I would like to get back to my book. I was just about to find out who the killer is."

"The butler did it."

"Way to ruin a book. Thanks a lot."

❖

Megan shifted from one foot to the other as she waited for someone to answer the door. She couldn't help but smile when Tara appeared, her hair pulled into a ponytail, apron covering her clothes. "Hi there."

Tara pulled her into a hug and gave her a quick kiss. "Hi yourself. Come in. It's freezing." They made their way to the kitchen.

The warm smell of—what was that, brownies?—greeted her. "I've got dessert going and was just about to put the meat in the oven."

"What can I do to help?" Megan slipped off her jacket.

"Sit and look pretty."

"And that is helping how?"

"It helps me more than you know." Tara took her jacket and hung it in the closet by the door. "My sister should be home soon. Sit." She waved a hand.

Megan sat but she wasn't convinced she was the pretty one, not when Tara looked so beautiful, even with her cheeks slightly red from the heat of the stove as she stirred something that released a plume of steam when she'd opened the lid.

Tara covered the pot and turned to Megan. "Wine?"

"I'll wait."

"Honey, I'm home." Megan turned to the voice behind her. The woman had hair a little lighter than Tara's and shared the same deep blue eyes. She was a little taller and just as slender. "You must be Megan," she said and held out a hand. "I'm Anna, Tara's sister."

Megan stood and shook the hand that was offered. "So nice to meet you. And this must be Brandon. How are you doing?"

"Good," he responded without making more than a second or two of eye contact.

"Your aunt Tara told me so much about you. It's good to finally meet you."

"Thanks." This time he held the eye contact a bit longer and a smile momentarily covered his face.

"Go wash up for supper?" his mother said, and he disappeared down the hall. "Tara's told me so much about you." Anna pulled out a chair and sat and Megan did the same.

"Good stuff, I hope."

"Some of it."

"Hey," Tara said. "It was all good. Mostly."

"I see your sister has your sense of humor. I can tell we're going to be friends," Megan said. She was rewarded with a smile from Anna and a matching one from Tara. It lit up her face, making her more beautiful. If that was even possible.

The evening went well, dinner was delicious, and the conversation was nonstop and interesting. It was fun to watch the interplay between Tara and Anna. It reminded Megan of her relationship with her own sister.

"I've never seen Brandon interact with someone he didn't know as much as he did with you," Tara said later when they were back at Megan's apartment, sitting close together on the couch. "He really liked you."

"I liked him. Anna too."

"Some people ignore him as if he isn't there or like he's stupid. He's not. He just doesn't have a lot of social skills. But you didn't. I appreciated that."

"Of course. We all have our weaknesses." She used air quotes. "His are just a little more visible."

"I love you," Tara said before she could stop the words from coming out of her mouth. She had a moment of panic as the words hung in the air between them.

Megan seemed to take several long beats to let it sink in. "I love you, too."

Tara was sorry she'd said anything. "You don't have to say that just because I did." The last thing she wanted was to make Megan feel like she needed to reciprocate.

"I wouldn't say it if it wasn't true." She tipped Tara's chin up and looked at her.

Tara felt like Megan was looking into her soul. She felt seen like she'd never felt before. So many feelings with Megan were new and exciting.

"I love you," Megan repeated. "I need you to believe it. You make me want to be the best me I can be. I love being with you. I hate it when we're apart, 'cause all I do is think about you."

The words went right to Tara's heart, circled around, and settled in. Yes, she believed Megan. How could she not? The connection between them was so strong that it felt like it would swallow her whole and she would go willingly.

"I know this is all so new," Megan said. "But it feels so right.

You know I've had relationships before. But, Tara, believe me when I say this is different. I wasn't looking for love, but I found it. And I don't ever want to let it—you—go." She raised her eyebrows and Tara assumed she was waiting for Tara's response.

"I feel exactly the same way about you."

Any other thoughts went immediately out of her head when Megan kissed her. Deeply. Passionately. Tara willingly parted her lips when Megan's tongue pressed against them seeking a deeper connection. She willingly gave her body to Megan as their clothes were shed and they made love on the couch, before moving to the floor and starting all over again.

Epilogue

"Will you come and look at a house with me today?" Tara asked Megan over the phone. Her divorce and settlement were final, and the money was just sitting in her bank account ready to use. And she was ready to get on with her life. Her sister had been more than generous, letting her stay as long as she needed, although she'd spent more time with Megan than with Anna. Which Anna didn't seem to mind, because Milton had all but moved in. Tara was so happy for them.

"Of course."

Tara didn't tell her that she'd already looked at several houses and had a favorite. She hoped that Megan would fall in love with it too. "I'll pick you up at five. You should be done with work by then, right? Does that work?"

"It does. I'll be ready."

Tara put her phone in the desk drawer as she waited for her students to start arriving. She spotted a hummingbird outside the window and watched as he fluttered about looking for the perfect flower. Spring had been late to arrive, but when it did, it came like a whirlwind, seemingly overnight. And summer was just a week away. The irises danced in the light breeze and the white snow that had blanketed the ground had long been replaced by bright green grass. She was riding high on life. Everything seemed to be going her way. She hoped that continued after Megan saw the house.

She turned when she heard a tiny voice call her name. "Mrs. Foreman."

She'd gone back to her maiden name but didn't want to confuse the children. She would introduce herself as Ms. Murry to next year's class. "Good morning," she said, going to the door. The little girl chose a fist bump as her way of greeting, and Tara was happy to oblige. The rest of the class trickled in, and her workday started.

Megan was waiting for her outside, sitting on the steps, when Tara pulled up. "Hello, my love," she said as she climbed into the car. She leaned in for a kiss, which Tara gladly gave her.

"How was your day?"

"Fine. Great, now that I'm with you."

"Aww. I feel the same," Tara said. She pulled out onto the road and turned in the direction of the house she'd fallen in love with. She hoped Megan felt the same. The For Sale sign swung slightly in the warm air.

"This is it," Tara said. She recognized the Realtor's car, already in the driveway. She pulled up next to it. "What do you think?"

"I really like the outside. The stonework is beautiful."

Tara liked it even better than the first time she looked at it. The front garden was coming to life and waking up with the warmth of the day.

They strolled up the sidewalk hand in hand and were greeted at the door by Frances. Tara made the introductions, and they made their way into the house. The large foyer reached up to the second floor, and the open stairway on the right boasted a polished oak banister. A beautiful chandelier hung from the ceiling. The large rooms were painted in muted colors with oak trim, and the cabinets in the kitchen were a pale gray on top and a darker shade of gray on the bottom.

"The appliances are all less than two years old," Frances announced. "And the counters are granite." She ran her hand over the kitchen island.

Tara watched Megan's face light up as they went from room to room. She seemed just as excited about the house as Tara was. "Don't you love this view?" Tara asked. The dining room had a large sliding glass door that led to a deck. Beyond that was a beautifully landscaped yard that bordered a wooded area filled with evergreens, birch, and several other types of trees. The sunlight filtered through the leaves, casting a warm glow on everything.

"It's beautiful," Megan responded.

They made their way upstairs, while Frances remained on the main floor. "Only three bedrooms, but we can make do with that," Tara said. She watched Megan's face to see if she had any reaction to the word "we." She didn't seem to. "The master bedroom." Tara waved her arm as if she was a model showing off a prize on a game show. "And check out the master bath. A tub, shower, two closets, and two sinks. One for each of us."

Megan looked at her and smiled. "This house is gorgeous."

They continued to the next room. "Smaller bedroom for the guest room."

Megan peered into the room, big enough for a queen-size bed and dresser.

"And this one can be your office," Tara said as they entered the last bedroom.

"My office?" Megan looked confused.

"Yes. Your office. And Dozer's litter box can go in the bathroom, there." Tara pointed across the hall.

Megan gave half a laugh. "Dozer doesn't usually accompany me on sleepovers."

"I know," Tara said. "I want you to live here with me. I want this to be *our* place. That is," she quickly added, "if you like it. If you don't, we can keep looking." As much as Tara loved the house, she loved Megan more. "What do you think?"

Megan seemed to be at a loss for words. Tara hoped that wasn't a bad sign. "So?"

"I love the house. And I love you. I would like nothing more than to live here and spend the rest of my life with you."

Tara smiled, as she looked at the woman who had somehow become both her anchor and her wings. "I love you too," she whispered. "So very much."

About the Author

Creativity for Joy Argento started young. She was only five, growing up in Syracuse, New York, when she picked up a pencil and began drawing animals. These days she calls Rochester home, and oil paints are her medium of choice. Her award-winning art has found its way into homes around the globe.

Writing came later in life for Joy. Her love of lesbian romance inspired her to try her hand at writing, and she found her first self-published novels well received. She is thrilled to be a part of the Bold Strokes family and has enjoyed their books for years.

Joy has three grown children who are making their own way in the world and seven grandkids who are the light of her life.

Books Available From Bold Strokes Books

Anywhere with You by Margo Glynn. On a road trip through the Great American Southwest, two friends discover nature, hope, and each other. (978-1-63679-907-0)

Burning Bridges by Lesley Davis. Can Clancy and Jude crack the case of eight missing women—and the secrets of their own hearts? (978-1-63679-872-1)

Dreams Entangled by Sophia Kell Hagin. Amid self-doubt, secrets, a pandemic, fear of attack and attempted murder, Pirin and Gracie's attraction turns to love, and their lives will never be the same. (978-1-63679-892-9)

Echoes of Love by Catherine Lane. As Hazel's and Jo's paths intertwine, they're swept up in a whirlwind of long-buried secrets, sizzling chemistry, and memories that won't be denied. (978-1-63679-835-6)

The Fame Game by Ronica Black. Wild child Hollywood actress Luna Kirkman begins dating Hollywood's leading man, only to fall for his straitlaced sister instead. (978-1-63679-858-5)

Moonlight Obsession by Sheri Lewis Wohl. All it takes to stop a clever killer is moonlight, love, and a silver bullet. (978-1-63679-831-8)

My Boyfriend's Wife by Joy Argento. Amid betrayal and heartbreak, can two women discover a love that could heal their pasts and rewrite their futures? (978-1-63679-866-0)

Tapout by Nicole Disney. A struggling MMA fighter finds her edge in an underground ring, but as she falls for the magnetic and ambitious promoter behind the matches, their dangerous world threatens to destroy everything they've fought to rebuild. (978-1-63679-924-7)

An Extraordinary Passion by Kit Meredith. An autistic podcaster must decide whether to take a chance on her polyamorous guest and indulge their shared passion, despite her history. (978-1-63679-679-6)

Heart's Appraisal by Jo Hemmingwood. Andy and Hazel can't deny their attraction, but they'll never agree on the place they call home. (978-1-63679-856-1)

That's Amore by Georgia Beers. The romantic city of Rome should inspire Lily's passion for writing, if she can look away from Marina Troiani, her witty, smart, and unassumingly beautiful Italian tour guide. (978-1-63679-841-7)

Through Sky and Stars by Tessa Croft. Can Val and Nicole's love cross space and time to change the fate of humanity? (978-1-63679-862-2)

Uncomplicate It by Kel McCord. When an office attraction threatens her career, Hollis Reed's carefully laid plans demand revision. (978-1-63679-864-6)

The Unexpected Heiress by Cassidy Crane. When a cynical opportunist meets a shy but spirited heiress, the last thing she plans is for her heart to get involved. (978-1-63679-833-2)

Vanguard by Gun Brooke. Beth Wild, Subterranean freedom fighter, is in the crosshairs when she fights for her people and risks her heart for loving the exacting Celestial dissident leader, LaSierra Delmonte. (978-1-63679-818-9)

Wild Night Rising by Barbara Ann Wright. Riding Harleys instead of horses, the Wild Hunt of myth is once again unleashed upon the world. Their ousted leader and a fey cop must join forces to rein in the ride of terror. (978-1-63679-749-6)

A Thousand Tiny Promises by Morgan Lee Miller. When estranged childhood friends Audrey and Reid reunite to fulfill their best friend's dying wish, the last thing they expect is a journey toward healing their broken friendship and discovering a newfound love for each other. (978-1-63679-630-7)

Behold My Heart by Ronica Black. Alora Anders is a highly successful artist who's losing her vision. Devastated, she hires Bodie Banks, a young struggling sculptor, as a live-in assistant. Can Alora open her mind and her heart to accept Bodie into her life? (978-1-63679-810-3)

Fearless Hearts by Radclyffe. One wounded woman, one determined to protect her—and a summertime of risk, danger, and desire. (978-1-63679-837-0)

www.ingramcontent.com/pod-product-compliance
Lightning Source LLC
Chambersburg PA
CBHW030521020726
47494CB00004B/1178